MW00460546

THE
UNDYING KING
A NOVELLA

Grace Draven

Copyright © 2009 by Grace Draven.

All rights reserved. No part of this publication may be reproduced, distributed or transmitted in any form or by any means, including photocopying, recording, or other electronic or mechanical methods, without the prior written permission of the publisher, except in the case of brief quotations embodied in critical reviews and certain other noncommercial uses permitted by copyright law. For permission requests, write to the publisher, addressed "Attention: Permissions Coordinator," at the address below.

Grace Draven
Grace.Draven1@gmail.com
www.gracedraven.com

Publisher's Note: This is a work of fiction. Names, characters, places, and incidents are a product of the author's imagination. Locales and public names are sometimes used for atmospheric purposes. Any resemblance to actual people, living or dead, or to businesses, companies, events, institutions, or locales is completely coincidental.

Book Layout ©2013 BookDesignTemplates.com
Cover Illustration © 2016 by Isis Sousa
Cover Layout Design by Isis Sousa

The Undying King/ Grace Draven
ISBN – 13: 978-1-1540446695
ISBN – 10: 1-540446697

For Mel and Lora, in the 11th hour.

Thank you.

CHAPTER ONE

Wrapped in concealing wool and tight gloves, Imogen slumped in her chair by the bedside and waited for her mother to die.

The air stank of old blood and sickness, made even more pungent by the sweltering heat generated by the fire in the hearth. She gazed at the room's single window edged in an early spring frost. The small hours before dawn passed in quiet darkness, and she imagined the coolness outside, the crisp scent of pine and the first hint of perfume from the white daffodils rising from lingering ribbons of snow on the low hillocks surrounding the dale.

Niamh loved daffodils, not for their herbal properties but simply for their beauty. Even now a generous spray of them stood in a pint mug on the rough-hewn table. Imogen had gathered them the previous day after chopping wood for the fire. She'd marveled at their pale petals against her black gloves. The few times Niamh had awakened from a pained sleep, she'd looked to the flowers and smiled weakly. Imogen swore she'd harvest every daffodil in the surrounding county if it meant her mother might forget, for just a moment, the agony wracking her wasted body.

1

A rattling exhalation signaled Niamh had woken. Light from a low candle standing on a nearby table cast dancing shadows across the bed and illuminated the sick woman's features.

Even now, after months of watching her mother waste away with illness, Imogen's shock at the ghastly change didn't diminish. Once tall and vibrant, with lush curves and a face so beautiful the local bards crafted poems in her honor, Niamh had withered to a shrunken wraith. The long red hair had whitened and thinned. Her sun-browned hands, so capable of brewing elixirs, wielding spells and comforting a small child, now clutched her blankets with claw-like fingers.

She gazed at Imogen, her eyes dull and dark with pain. "Imogen, get the locked box on the shelf," she commanded in a harsh whisper.

Imogen caressed Niamh's forehead with a gloved hand. "Your tea's ready, Mother. That first."

Niamh captured her hand in an unyielding clasp, and her eyes, dim just a moment before, glittered feverishly in the candle's light. "Later. Now do what I say. Bring me the box." Desperation lent strength to her voice.

Puzzled by Niamh's sudden obsession with a forgotten box, Imogen gently pried her hand loose. "All right. Calm down. I'll get the box. Then tea, yes?"

Exhausted by the small exertion, Niamh nodded weakly and plucked restlessly at her blankets. Imogen fluffed her pillows and eased her patient into a sitting position. She inhaled at the sight of small blood spots blossoming on the blanket covering Niamh's thighs.

This was no woman's monthly moon but another manifestation of the illness consuming Niamh from the inside. Last week her gums had started bleeding.

"Imogen." Niamh's eyes held a gallows' humor. "You keep getting distracted. The box. Please."

The item creating such a stir sat on the shelf near the frosted window, its lid coated in dust. Imogen lifted it from the shelf and wiped the surface with the hem of her shift, leaving a gritty smear on the delicate trim.

A plain container made of old oak, the box held no visual interest save a lock with no key. She returned to Niamh's bedside and placed it in her trembling hands.

"I didn't see a key on the shelf."

"That's because I'm the key." Niamh's thin fingers traced the lock's outline, and she murmured arcane words of spellwork.

Her whispers worked their magic. The lock clicked twice before springing open. Seeing Niamh didn't need any help with the box, Imogen quickly lost interest and turned her attention to the kettle and cup waiting on the table.

Niamh's pain was almost constant now and growing more severe by the day. Imogen had used up their supply of crushed valerian root and was fast working her way through the skullcap and St. John's wort to make the teas Niamh consumed by the kettle full. She took little else, despite Imogen's combined tactics of threats and coaxing to eat a little chicken broth.

"Ah, there it is! The key to unlock the greatest of gates."

Imogen didn't look up from pouring the hot water in the cup so the leaves might steep. "I hope it was worth waiting for your tea. This will take a few minutes to cool."

"Don't be such a shrew, girl. Come here and see what I have for you."

When Imogen resumed her seat by the bed, Niamh handed her a finely stitched book made of supple leather and expensive parchment yellowed with age. A sheen of tears brightened her eyes, and Imogen's heart jumped in her chest.

"What's wrong?"

Niamh's melancholy smile matched her teary gaze. She curled her fingers around Imogen's gloved ones. "Nothing that time and a little reading can't fix." She released her daughter's hand to stroke the book's cover. "You are my child in every way save blood and birthright."

Imogen's heart continued to thump hard against her ribs. The sickness had changed Niamh physically, almost beyond recognition, but not her mind. Until now. Imogen didn't know what to make of the suddenly maudlin creature clutching her hands despite the danger, and her grief grew a hundred fold. Time was growing very short for Niamh of Leids.

"When you were small, I told you all the stories of the Berberi kingdom. Do you remember?"

Imogen nodded. She'd been raised on tales of King Varn and his court, the great markets in the capital city, the library and theaters, the grand avenues on which the aristocracy strolled to see and be seen. It was another world, as far away and inaccessible as the moon. As a young child, Imogen had listened to Niamh's recounting of such things with wide eyes and gone to bed dreaming of lavish courts and beautiful princesses courted by noble princes.

Those dreams had gone the way of other childhood fascinations as she grew to womanhood. Burdened as she was with a curse she'd carried since birth, she would never marry or be courted by either prince or nobleman. Not even a farmer or swineherd.

Like Imogen, Niamh had put aside those tales and concentrated on teaching the things that guaranteed survival—the knowledge of herbs, the brewing of draughts and elixirs, the harvesting of wild roots and berries, and the construction and placements of traps. Even those things came second to grueling lessons in languages, with letters learned by scratching in the dirt and reading the same six books Niamh owned until Imogen had memorized them from cover to cover.

Only twice had she seen this particular book. Once, when Imogen was twelve, she'd found Niamh scribbling madly in the pages and then again a year ago, when she first showed signs of illness. She hadn't offered any explanation, and Imogen didn't ask. Nothing could force her mother to reveal her secrets or motivations until she was ready, and the time had not come until now.

Niamh continued to stroke the book. "This was a gift. From King Varn."

Imogen stared at the book with new eyes. When had Niamh consorted with a Berberi king?

"Ha! I knew that would chase the boredom off your face." Niamh's grin revealed bloodied gums and teeth stained scarlet. The grin faded. "I've not lied outright to you, Imogen, but I've withheld much from you—things you've a right to know—things I should have told you long ago were I not such a coward."

Alarmed as much by claims of cowardice as she was by Niamh's bloody mouth, Imogen rose. "Your tea should be cooled now." She pointed a finger to halt Niamh's protest and straightened her blankets.

"Not another word, Mother. We bargained, you and I. The box and then the tea. You have your box. Now you'll have your tea. And no more foolish talk of cowards."

She returned with the warm tea and held the cup as Niamh sipped and dabbed her dry lips with a soft cloth. The cloth came away spotted red. Both women stared at the stains for a few moments before Niamh spoke.

"We both know I've little time left to me. I should have done this sooner." She handed the book to Imogen. "This book is for you. Recipes I didn't have the time to teach you, bits and pieces of a life lived and mistakes made, discoveries of wonder." Tears edged her eyelids. "Recollections of your childhood."

With those words, the book grew heavier in Imogen's hands. Like Niamh, she caressed the book reverently. She met her mother's dark stare. "Why would you say such things make you a coward?"

Niamh's gaze never wavered. "Because they aren't what you need to know most, and some misdeeds are too painful to write down or speak of, including the origins of your curse." She shushed Imogen's protests. "Listen to me. Promise you'll read the book when I'm gone and remember that I loved you as my own." She clutched Imogen's gloved hand. "Swear it."

"I swear."

Seemingly satisfied with Imogen's answer, she fell back against the pillow, her pallid features blanching the color of sun-bleached bone. "Look in the box. There's a trinket there, a thing far costlier than a treasure house full of gold."

Shaken, Imogen reached into the box and lifted out a piece of silver jewelry. It looked like nothing more than a noblewoman's lost pendant on a delicate chain. Fine workmanship and far more valuable than anything she or Niamh owned but certainly not unique and not equal to the gold in a treasure house. She touched it, and a shock of vibration shot up her arm so strong, she yelped. The pendant sat heavy and warm in her hand, weightier than its appearance suggested. The strange vibrations continued to pulse along her fingers through her gloves. Raised by a witch of Niamh's caliber, Imogen didn't startle easily at the odd and sometimes frightening manifesting before her, but she inhaled when the intricate knotwork within the symbol moved, reforming in serpentine motion until a new pattern took shape.

She glanced at Niamh who smiled in satisfaction. "What think you of that piece?"

The pendant felt alive, not because of its movements but simply for its presence. Imogen wondered if she held it up to her ear, if it might whisper some dark secret.

"Well?" Niamh's question interrupted her thoughts.

"I don't know. It's strange, touched by magic but none like yours."

Niamh's enigmatic laughter ended on a hiss of pain. She waved away Imogen's solicitous hand. "Stop hovering. The pain will fade soon enough." Once she caught her breath again, her voice trembled. "That is the map and the key to the gates of Tineroth."

Imogen frowned, growing more certain Niamh's suffering affected her mind. Tineroth and her sister city Mir were nothing more than fables, stories to entertain around the fire and moral lessons on the corruptive ruin of absolute power.

A flutter in her palm distracted her. The pendant writhed into a new mold, as if hearing the word "Tineroth" had awakened it from a half slumber. She almost leapt out of her chair when Niamh touched the pendant, and a silver metal tendril rose to wrap around her finger like a living vine.

"This is the key to your salvation, Imogen. And maybe, just maybe, my redemption."

Imogen overcame the urge to drop the pendant and wipe her hand against her shift. "Mother," she said evenly. "Where did you get this thing?"

"It was a gift of thanks. From a man to whom I once offered succor during a time of terrible suffering. He said if I ever needed him, to use this key. It would lead me to Tineroth. You must go there." Niamh's eyes clouded. "I'd hoped to take you there myself, but it's too late now." She rubbed the tendril of silver with her thumb before twirling her finger to release it. It rose in the air as if seeking her and finally coiled back to entwine with its stiller mates.

Whatever mage-born spell had animated the trinket, Imogen was sure it had not been one laid by a local witch. Its power was ancient, and it both drew and repelled her.

Had she not seen for herself the pendant's strange movements, she might have thought Niamh's statements regarding Tineroth nothing more than the mutterings of an ill, hallucinatory woman, but she couldn't deny what her eyes saw and her gloved hand felt.

"The stories say Tineroth and Mir vanished thousands of years ago. You would have me travel to some place that no longer exists?"

Niamh coughed and winced, her once beautiful face haggard. "The pendant will lead you straight there. Those with the Blessed Eye have sometimes recounted sightings of Tineroth when the day is longest in summer and the shadows fall thin on the ground. The pendant will be your Eye."

Imogen didn't relish the thought of journeying into unknown lands alone looking for a fabled city. So far, Niamh had only made her swear to read her journal. She hoped she wouldn't have to promise to set off on some fool's journey. She offered more of the skullcap and wort tea

Niamh refused. "I'm heartily sick of drinking that swill. Let me finish." Her thin fingers worried a pulled threat on one of her blankets. "Tineroth is still ruled by its king—Cededa, son of Hamarath the Younger."

The pendant suddenly unfurled from its many knots, and Imogen gasped, nearly spilling the tea when metal ribbons rose to stand at attention in her palm. They began to sway, silver serpents dancing to the unheard tune of a snake charmer. Just as quickly they collapsed and melded for a third time into a new shape.

A tired chuckle escaped Niamh's mouth. "You see? Even now, the trinket recognizes the name of its master."

Imogen's upper lip curled, and she lifted the pendant gingerly by its silver chain. Her hand twitched, an involuntary cupping as if to recapture its treasure. She shuddered and dropped the trinket unceremoniously in the box. It struck the bottom with a thump, and both women heard a soft but clear hiss of protest before Imogen slammed the box closed.

"I can't concentrate when that thing is constantly jumping up and down in my hand like a trapped spider." She wiped imaginary dust off her gloves and resumed her seat. "You were saying?"

Niamh's affectionate smile reminded Imogen of better days. "You were always a squeamish one when it came to insects and worms."

"It's the crawly little legs I don't like. I always have the urge to scratch, like now." She smoothed the blankets over Niamh's thin legs and was relieved to see the small blood spots had not spread. "Continue with your tale."

"It's no tale, girl, but the truth. Tineroth is real as is her king. His people once called him Cededa the Fair, then Cededa the Butcher, and then they called him no more. Only the carvings on Tineroth's gates remember him and not by name. He drank the Waters and became the Undying King."

Chills spread across Imogen's body despite the room's stifling heat. She knew the story of the Undying King, an emperor desperate to retain his throne and his power who drank the Waters of Eternal Life. That which should have been a blessing had become a curse.

His true name had been lost in the passage of time and the births and deaths of generations. The idea that a man so old still lived and lingered in an ancient city seen only by ensorcelled eyes raised goose flesh on her arms. That Niamh knew his true name and wanted to send her daughter to him made her shiver.

"He is a great warrior, but most importantly, a great mage," Niamh continued, ignoring her daughter's growing unease. She reached for Imogen who clasped her hand. "He can break your curse, Imogen. I know it!" The fervor in her voice was reflected in the glitter of her eyes. "When I am gone, you must find Tineroth and Cededa. Tell him you've come to call in a debt owed. The Waters have cursed him with long life and blessed him with great power. He can do for you what I never could, no matter how hard I tried."

The strength with which Niamh squeezed her hand surprised Imogen and alarmed her. "Peace, Mother." She bathed the woman's sweating brow, feeling the dampness soak into her glove and wishing she might comfort her with a bare hand instead of one covered in protective shrouding. "Be still. That's enough excitement for now."

But Niamh refused to quiet. "Don't patronize me, girl," she wheezed. "I'm not dead yet." Her dark stare threatened to burn holes in Imogen. "Do you understand what I'm saying? Cededa can give you the life you should have had. No more gloves or isolation." Her voice faded, and her eyelids drooped as the tea's mild narcotic effects finally took hold. "A life no longer held prisoner by death." She said the last on a sigh and fell asleep.

Imogen held vigil for a moment before rising to dump the rest of the cup's contents into the fire. The flame sizzled and hissed, reminding her of the enchanted pendant in the box. Her thoughts whirled in a soup of confusion and burgeoning hope. She ruthlessly crushed the second, consigning it to the deep recesses of her mind where other false dreams and dead hopes resided. No one—not even an immortal king—could rid her of this malevolence lurking beneath her skin. Imogen doubted she'd receive either aid or mercy from a man whose own people christened him The Butcher.

But Niamh believed in Cededa of Tineroth, and Imogen believed in Niamh. The hope she'd driven back into the shadows refused to go quietly and rose up to float beneath the surface of her more mundane thoughts, lingering there as she brewed a cup of tea for herself and sat at the table admiring daffodils in the guttering firelight. Could an immortal king truly help a woman who'd been born as Death's handmaiden?

Niamh's steady, if frail, breathing comforted her, lulling her into a waking daze where the pop of burning wood and the shifting creak of tree branches outside played a lyrical tune. In the loft, her bed lay empty, the sheets stale and cold. Imogen hadn't slept there the past four days and her back was beginning to feel the strain of sleeping in her hard chair, but she refused to leave Niamh's side. She yawned, folded her arms on the table and rested her head on their makeshift pillow. She was asleep in moments and dreamed of silver serpents twining about her legs and arms in a cool, metallic caress. Their scales were slippery smooth and glided over her skin in whispers, like sands shifting on an ancient shore.

A rattling gasp awakened her just as the first red streaks of dawn painted the window. She jerked upright, befuddled with sleep. Her gaze settled on the bed where Niamh's entire body convulsed and arched beneath blankets soaked in gore from waist to knee.

Imogen raced to the bedside. "Oh gods; oh gods," she chanted as she gripped Niamh's thin shoulders to hold her still. Her mother heaved under her hands, eyes rolled back into her head, mouth wet with blood-flecked spittle.

The thrashing seemed to go on forever. Niamh finally calmed, her sunken eyes still closed in a face made cadaverous and paler than marble. Her breath rattled, pausing in spaces of silence so long Imogen wondered if she had finally slipped the bonds that held her spirit to earth. But Niamh held on—long enough to open her eyes and gaze at her daughter with a pleading expression that made Imogen flinch. "Forgive me, my darling girl," she rasped.

Imogen stared into those dark, dark eyes with all their memories and secrets and saw surrender. Death was a shadow on the doorstep, one foot already across the threshold, held at bay only by the pain that gripped her mother. Tears spilled down Imogen's cheeks, dripping on to their entwined fingers. "Oh Mother, there's nothing to forgive."

"Help me, Imogen. I am so very tired."

Imogen gasped out a sob. She released Niamh long enough to remove her gloves. Ivory hands, smooth and unblemished by scars or the sun lifted and meshed slowly with Niamh's own wrinkled ones, their clasp as lethal as it was merciful.

The older woman smiled gently. For a moment her gaze sharpened, grew clear with wonder. Imogen, caught in that same wonder and bittersweet sorrow of touching her mother's skin for the first time without gloves, leaned forward and kissed Niamh's cool forehead. When she straightened, Niamh still wore the smile, but her eyes were blank.

Heedless of the bloody linens, Imogen gathered the limp, fragile body into her arms and greeted the dawn with quiet sobs.

CHAPTER TWO

The descending sun lacquered the Adal harbor in crimson and orange light. From his place at one of the high windows in his library, Prince Hayden watched ships sail slowly into the harbor, accompanied by playful dolphins that rode the slow-treading bow waves. Dwellings clung to the cliff walls on either side of the harbor, their walking paths snaking down the worn rock like ribbons in a woman's hair. The white-washed walls of houses gleamed in the dying light, and lanterns flickered to life amidst the rise of shadows.

The young prince ignored the picturesque scene before him. He'd viewed it a thousand times, and its glory was lost on him. Instead, he looked beyond the harbor, to the vast sea that swelled with the rising tide and the coming of nightfall. There, past the horizon and out of his reach, were the shipping lanes that provided wealth and riches untold to the neighboring kingdom of Berberi. Hayden's hands clenched into fists. Those shipping lanes rightfully belonged to the kingdom of Castagher, and if she had the martial power Berberi did, Hayden would wrest them from Berberi by force.

His hands relaxed. There were other ways to gain back what was lost, ways that didn't require war and bloodshed. He had no wish to be the king his father had been, bankrupting his country to finance wars that only weakened Castagher in the end.

A polite knock at the door signaled his awaited visitor had arrived. "Enter," he called.

Dradus, Castagher's highest ranking mage and Hayden's most trusted advisor, bowed briefly. His sly gaze lit on the prince before passing over the new texts he'd sent from the library of a mage condemned for heresy.

"I see you received my gifts, Sire."

Hayden turned away from the window to face him. "I did. They are fine indeed. I've only had a chance to browse through one of them so far." He waved his hand as if to brush off the topic. "That is unimportant. What have you discovered?"

Dradus rubbed his palms together. "It is as the servant said. Old Varn's mistress didn't disappear. She simply moved to the Borders. Folks from three of the nearby towns said a red-haired witch named Niamh traded with them at market day. The older ones remember her carrying a baby, always swaddled, that she let no one touch or see."

"Varn's daughter."

"I'm almost sure of it."

Hayden scowled. "You need to be absolutely certain, Dradus. I want the girl found and brought back here. If she's Varn's offspring, then I will have rightful access to those shipping lanes."

Dradus hesitated in delivering his next bit of news. "My scouts think they've found the home where the witch lives. A hovel away from the main road and even the cattle path. The villagers say two women live there, but both are old."

"Sounds like the wrong hovel then."

The mage shook his head. "Not necessarily. Niamh possessed strong magic and could manipulate illusion. She might have magicked the girl to look like a crone. It's said one of them always wore gloves and refused to touch anything offered to her in the market."

Hayden closed his eyes and pinched the bridge of his nose. There was more conjecture in Dradus's story than real information, but he couldn't afford to take any chances and lose a scent. For almost thirty years, Niamh had managed to avoid capture by both Dradus and his father. That she hadn't already slipped through his fingers surprised him. "Any of your scouts mages like you?"

"Only one and no match for a witch of Niamh's skill." Dradus executed a small bow. "With your permission, I can ride there with a small troop and bring the girl back to you if she proves to be Varn's."

Hayden arched a skeptical eyebrow. "It takes a troop of soldiers and a mage-adept to bring in an old woman and a girl?"

Dradus's features smoothed into an expressionless mask. "Think of it more as a powerful witch and her trained apprentice, Sire."

The mage had a point. "Fine. Take as many soldiers as you deem necessary. I want her captured and brought to me."

"Sire, rumor has it she may be cursed or diseased."

Hayden shrugged. "I don't care if she's half eaten with leprosy. I need only prove she's Varn's daughter and my betrothed and those shipping lanes are mine."

Dradus bowed low and backed out of the room, leaving Hayden alone with his thoughts once more. A dying nursemaid who had sought to unburden her soul in hopes of redemption had been an unexpected boon for him. Varn's daughter and his dead aunt's child. He wondered briefly whom she might resemble then shrugged the thought away. It mattered little. She was a child of Berberi and Castagher, and the means by which Hayden intended to extract just due from his neighbor.

CHAPTER THREE

The ancient fir that stood sentinel over Niamh's grave had borne silent witness to a few of the spring and autumnal rituals the witch performed when she lived. Imogen thought it fitting the tree watch over her mother's body where it lay buried beneath black earth and a mound of stones.

Niamh had died a week earlier, and the daffodils she so admired spread across the forest floor in a vast white and yellow tapestry. Imogen set a spray of the flowers atop the grave and bowed her head.

"It's very quiet now, Mother. I miss you."

As if in answer, a zephyr wind smelling of rye and apple blossoms blew across her shoulders, fluttering the tendrils of dark hair that had escaped her plait. A fanciful indulgence it might be, but she liked to think Niamh's spirit lingered where her body rested, if only to greet Imogen when she visited the grave each day.

Some might think it strange that she came each afternoon to sit by the grave and talk to a pile of rocks, but Imogen didn't care. Niamh had been her only companion her entire life, the one person who shared conversation with her. Her grief was still too fresh to give that up now, even if Niamh never replied.

Imogen fished in her apron pocket and pulled out the journal her mother had given her the night of her death. She kept it with her these days, reading it, as promised, during spare moments between chores and in the evening just before bed. The journal revealed a Niamh Imogen had never known or imagined.

The ground beneath her was dry and sun-warmed as she sat down cross-legged next to the grave and removed her gloves. Imogen liked to read here best, with the spirit of her mother close by and her memories revealing themselves in a flowing scrawl of faded ink.

Recipes for elixirs occupied the pages alongside lists of spells and commentary on the politics of the Berberi court. The spells and recipes were familiar. After hours of lessons and singing repetitious songs with ingredients and chants as lyrics, she knew them by heart.

But it was her mother's observations of the vagaries of the aristocrats that captured Imogen's interest. Astute, observant Niamh; she'd been less than impressed with the shenanigans perpetrated by spoiled, entitled nobility.

Imogen had gone wide-eyed at the discovery that Niamh had once been the pampered mistress of King Varn, and she blushed as she read those entries. Niamh waxed poetic and graphically about Varn's physical prowess.

He is a fine man, the king. Strong shoulders and hair like the sun at Solstice. I see the women of court eye him. He's a prized stallion and not just for his wealth and power. If they only knew the man was hung as well as the biggest stud in the royal stables.

"Honestly, Mother, was it necessary to write it down?" Imogen had muttered to herself and quickly skimmed the pages containing Niamh's descriptions of bed play. Her sharp, no-nonsense words echoed in Imogen's mind.

"The coupling between a man and a woman is as natural as it gets, Imogen. There's no shame to it, nor should it be whispered of furtively in the dark. That way lies ignorance and stupidity." She had blithely ignored Imogen's red face and proceeded to tell her in detail the mating rituals of man and woman.

It was years since that conversation, and Imogen still squirmed in embarrassment. Her mother explaining in her blunt fashion the way a lover should treat his mate was one thing, reading about such very personal experiences something else entirely. She fluttered those pages through her fingers until she reached the section she'd stopped at a day earlier. This entry was different and far more intriguing.

There is a man in my house. Or half a man at least. Poor creature. I stumbled upon him behind the bailey, hidden by the old rowan near the eastern wall. I thought him a half-rotten corpse, dug up from a shallow grave by an opportunistic scavenger. Then it spoke. Sweet gods, I nearly pissed myself.

Imogen worried her lower lip with two fingers, eyes glued to the page.

I almost left him there. My magic is of earth and seasons and growing things. I don't truck with the black mages of Westerwall, and this deathless horror facing me is surely the creation of one of these mages.

Imogen paused in her reading. The irony of Niamh's statements struck home. She wondered if the woman had ever reread these passages in her later years and thought to herself how strange it was that Death in another form resided in her house and had been raised at her knee.

She returned to her reading and Niamh's account of bringing the man into her house and placing him in one of the guest rooms where servants dared not visit. Planning and secrets and the need to keep down servant gossip made for good reading and Imogen was absorbed by her mother's descriptions of her patient. *He rarely speaks. I think the suffering is so great, it's too much effort to talk. I cannot help but watch as his body is slowly made whole by unseen hands. He must have been burned at some point, for it is ashes, still smelling of the fires, which swirl into the room and cast themselves upon him, becoming healthy flesh.*

Imogen's skin prickled at the imagery her descriptions evoked, and the hairs at her nape stood on end at the next entry.

I found a bone outside his door this morning, scorched black in spots. I don't know how it got here without being noticed. I didn't dare touch it, only opened the door and walked away. When I came to check on him in the afternoon, he had regained an arm."

Another entry referenced the Tineroth pendant.

This magic is old. Old beyond the memory of our books and scribes, even beyond the knowledge of the Primus mages. A key and a map to vanished Tineroth. There is truth in every legend. I didn't refuse the gift, though I have no desire to wear this strange bauble, nor any reason to seek this mad king's help. He speaks little even now, but his eyes...I will be glad to see him go back to whatever so desperately calls him."

Imogen rubbed her arms. She promised Niamh she would read her journal. She'd made no promise to seek out Cededa of Tineroth. Her hands, ungloved now, looked innocent enough, and she held them up, watching as sunbeams streamed between her fingers. Not until Niamh's death had she ever touched another living person with her bare hands. Her affliction might have been easier to shoulder if it was limited to her hands, but death flowed in her veins. Could this king, immune to the very thing that cursed her, truly help?

The light had grown so weak, Imogen had to squint to see the writing. She closed the book and rose from her place. The flowers resting atop the grave waved their petals at her in the gentle breeze, as if to bid her farewell for the evening. Imogen lifted the book and gazed speculatively at the burial mound. "Who is this woman I'm reading about, Mother? She is a stranger to me." Only the creak of the fir's limbs and the growing chorus of frogs peeping answered her. She returned the book to her apron pocket and trudged back to the house.

Her dinner that night might well have been a bowl of mud for all the attention she paid to it. Niamh's history, in the time before Imogen was born, read like the legends she'd filled her ears with in childhood. Lover of one man, savior to another. What had brought her so low in her later years?

Her gaze drifted to the box that still housed the Tineroth pendant. It rested back on its shelf undisturbed. Imogen had left the pendant alone, still unnerved by its odd abilities to come alive at unexpected moments. Her growing curiosity overrode her wariness, and she retrieved the box. Left unlocked by Niamh's spell, the lid opened easily, revealing the pendant. A metallic wink greeted Imogen, and she carefully lifted the bauble by its delicate chain and held it aloft.

It swung from her fingers, silver catching the candlelight so that it shimmered. At some point, after Imogen dropped it back in the box, the pendant had again reconfigured itself. The serpentine knotwork was now a lacy filigree that reminded her of crossing paths and roads that led to endless loops.

She eyed it closely. Keys bore many designs, especially magical ones. Set within the hidden spot of a wall or inserted into a decorative urn, any lock might open with the key made to match it. But a map as well? That was more of a puzzle, and Niamh's journal had yet to reveal that small secret.

The pendant half rotated one way and then the other on its chain as Imogen admired its new shape. Except for the eerie propensity to shift and writhe, the key was a thing of beauty, made to catch the eye of woman or man. Despite her misgivings and coaxed by an urging she couldn't explain, she slipped the chain over her head.

The silver lay warm against her breastbone, and Imogen wondered anew at the magic that made something so delicate in appearance feel so weighty. Wanting to see how the pendant looked on her, she opened the blanket chest at the foot of Niamh's bed and pulled out an ornate hand mirror.

Backed in silver decorated with curving designs of scrolls and roses, the mirror had been an endless source of temptation and at least two swats to the backside when Imogen was growing up. Using it to play pretend-I'm-a-queen had consequences.

Niamh, usually generous to a fault in accommodating her only child's wishes, had been uncharacteristically territorial with the mirror and had punished Imogen for sneaking it out of the blanket chest. She'd never explained her possessiveness, and after a second paddling and early trip to bed without supper for her transgression, Imogen lost any desire to ask why. Now, years later, with Niamh's journal to enlighten her, she suspected the mirror had been a treasured gift from King Varn.

She lifted the glass and eyed her reflection. Hers was a forgettable face and one only Niamh had seen as it actually was. Strong enchantments fooled everyone else into seeing an old woman who might have been Niamh's mother instead of her daughter. Imogen looked beyond the pale skin and brown hair to the pendant resting against her collarbones.

A truly lovely piece. She traced the new design with one finger, waiting to see if the pendant would do as it had with Niamh and wrap a silver tendril around her knuckle. It didn't move but sent small vibrations across the surface of her skin.

Imogen jerked her hand away as silver threads of lace suddenly unraveled and spread across her chest like a contagion of climbing ivy. Imogen's admiration turned to terror, and she cried out as the metal strands slithered up her neck and over her shoulders beneath her shirt. The mirror fell from her hand, shattering glass across the floor as she clawed at her skin.

The crawling feeling halted just below her jaw, and her flesh stung where her nails had torn at the metal tendrils. "Oh gods," she breathed. "What is this? What is this?" She ran her hand over what was now a filigreed collar and came away with a bloodied palm.

Heedless of the glass crunching beneath her shoes, she wrenched the door opened and stumbled outside—only to be greeted by a world gone topsy-turvy. What should have been a blanketing darkness that concealed anything beyond the weak corona of light spilling from her open door, was instead a shimmering miasma of illumination, as if thousands of fireflies swarmed the clearing around the cottage and the dark forest beyond.

Imogen gasped and blinked. Surely, she'd been made either blind or mad by the parasite encircling her neck and shoulders. But no amount of blinking diminished the lighted mist, and like the pendant, it began to take a defined shape. Vaporous, it coalesced into rigid lines that widened to create a single brightly lit path leading straight into the heart of the forest.

She backed into the house and slammed the door. The action dulled the brightness from outside but didn't shut it out. The illuminated path started at the tip of her toes. Imogen took two steps back and the path followed, moving where she did as if tethered to her feet.

Imogen breathed hard, grasping for a measure of calm and some small understanding of what just happened. Oh gods, why did she have to put on that cursed pendant? "Foolish, Imogen," she snarled. "How could you be so stupid?"

A tingling spread, sliding across her neck and shoulders, and she whimpered. The collar was growing again. She touched a spot below her neck and shuddered. The metal was gone, leaving in its place raised scars that mimicked its design. The tingling remained, not painful but unpleasant in a crawling, prickling way. Imogen bent and retrieved a shard of the mirror.

Sure enough, the reflection confirmed what she'd felt. The metal no longer shone as bright silver markings. Instead, it had melded into her skin, becoming part of her, leaving only a decorative scar marred by blood and scratches.

It was in her. Her heart banged against her ribs. Dear gods, whatever that thing was Niamh had received from the Tineroth mage-king, it had come alive and invaded her daughter. The thinnest thread holding Imogen's panic at bay snapped. A high whine grew in her ears, and her vision narrowed to a single point that blurred with tears. She ripped at her clothes and her skin, weeping as she tried to claw the pendant out of her body.

"Get it out!" she shrieked to the silent walls. "Get it out!"

From a far distance, she thought she heard Niamh's voice, stern, calming. *"Stop it, Imogen."*

Respect and obedience for her mother came as second nature, and Imogen immediately halted her frantic dance of wounding and mutilation. She breathed hard, swiping at the tears dripping down her cheeks, leaving blood smears behind.

"Mother?" she called feebly. Silence answered her, but that one moment, when Imogen was sure she'd heard Niamh's voice, broke the terror's hold on her.

She inhaled slowly, regaining a measure of calm. The sharp pain of the scratches on her neck cleared her head a little more.

"One problem at a time, Imogen," she told herself and set about heating water and laying out clean towels on the table. A bottle of lavender oil joined the supplies and soon she sat down at the table, hissing her misery each time she cleaned one of the scratches on her neck or chest and applied the oil.

The scratches, though painful, weren't deep, and she'd been careful to clean them thoroughly, despite the discomfort. She had every faith in the lavender oil she'd extracted last summer. Lavender was a good wound healer, and Niamh had sworn by its medicinal properties.

The mirror still lay in pieces on the floor, shards reflecting the gold-lit path that still ran from Imogen's feet and passed under the cottage door. A dull ache settled in the pit of her stomach. "Mother, if you rise from the earth this night to redden my backside for my carelessness, I won't be in the least surprised. I am so sorry."

She stood, cleared the table and set to sweeping the floor clean of the mirror's remains. The strange tingling under her skin had lessened but also expanded to other parts of her body, an ever-present reminder something now shared space with the curse inside her. Revulsion surged into her throat, carried on a stream of bile that she fought down with effort.

A key and a map to vanished Tineroth.

Niamh's flowing script replayed in her mind's eye, and Imogen paused in her sweeping. How did one find a city that had vanished thousands of years earlier? She glanced down at her feet and the luminescent path. One looked with ensorcelled eyes.

She groaned and rested her forehead on the tip of the broom handle. "Ah, Mother. You might have warned me."

The pendant wasn't the key or the map to Tineroth; she was. It had only served as the trigger to activate a spell, one created by a mage-king and given with his blessing to an unwitting witch who'd bequeathed it to her unknowing daughter. Imogen's disbelief in the Undying King's ability to break her curse didn't matter now. She had to seek him out simply to extract his nasty little artifact from her body and restore her eyesight to normal.

A simmering rage settled in her already queasy stomach, and she wielded the broom against the pile of broken glass as if it were a weapon. "Just wait until we meet, Sire. The second you get this thing out of me, I'm going to make you eat it."

CHAPTER FOUR

Since she'd have to travel to Tineroth on foot, she packed light, stuffing only the basic supplies into her knapsack – a wool blanket to keep her warm at night, dried rations to keep her fed, and two flasks of waters in case she traveled far from a water source. She tucked a small coin purse in her bodice and strapped a skinning knife to the belt at her waist. Niamh's journal found safe haven in a pocket of her cloak. The cloak would be a hindrance as she traveled through the forest, but Imogen never went without it if she ventured from the safety of their plot of land. It concealed her from head to toe in faded black, and without Niamh's protective illusion spells, she needed it now more than ever. With her wide-brimmed, veiled hat, a sturdy walking stick in her hand and an affected hobble, she looked like an old widowed crone. Poor, sickly, and of no interest to anyone. Or so Imogen hoped.

The gold light running from her feet to some unknown, distant place beckoned her. She shrugged the knapsack over her shoulder, grabbed the rowan walking stick from the corner and shut the cottage door behind her. "Let's get this over with," she said and set off toward the glade, following the path that took her from everything familiar.

She made one brief stop at Niamh's grave. The daffodils she'd left yesterday still looked freshly picked, and clusters of new grass blades peeked out between the crevices made by the stacked stone.

By summer, the mound would be covered, a low green hill that housed the bones of the witch whose magic originated from the earth.

Imogen pulled back her veil, grateful for the cool breeze drifting across her too-warm skin. "A prayer to the gods for me, Mother, that your indebted king will remember your kindness to him." She blew a kiss at the stones and set off for Tineroth.

After three days of trekking through the dense wood as she followed a path she suspected had doubled back on itself at least twice, she finally reached a deep gorge. The late afternoon sun sank below the trees behind her, casting sentinel shadows that stretched to the edge of the cliffs. Even this high up, Imogen heard the dull roar of water rushing below. She peered over the edge of the rock on which she stood to see the rope of a river snaking along the bottom of the gorge.

A powerful wind roared up from the yawning space, snapping her heavy braid like a whip. The gold path that had led her through dense woods and across fallow fields now stretched across the divide, cleaving a spectral road in thin air to the other side. A gathering darkness waited there, shaped by tall silhouettes rising out of ground fog that seemed to swirl with odd purpose.

Too tired to be frightened, Imogen groaned and rubbed the dull ache at her lower back. "Please tell me I don't have to climb down this cliff to stay on the path." Vertigo made her back away from her precarious perch, and she stared at the illuminated road, vexed by this sudden dilemma. "A key, a map and a road." Her fingers traced the raised scars on her neck. "Can you be a bridge now? Or maybe a bird?"

As if in answer, a ripple of movement flowed down the golden path, rising in shimmers like summer heat off hot stone. Imogen squinted and stared harder, hoping what she saw was not a trick of the fading light but one of the pendant's magic.

A bridge formed, stone by stone and stretched across the abyss like a giant's broken ribcage, choked by weeds and climbing vines. A series of arches perforated by spandrels at its ends, the bridge looked as if it grew from the cliff face itself, a living anchor that bound the earth together and trapped the river below it. The bridge deck, constructed of pavers, looked wide enough to accommodate a heavy flow of carts and foot traffic. Parapets lined its edges, decorated at intervals with statues that stood watch over crowds and visitors who had long since disappeared.

Still wary of the pendant's power and her altered eyesight, Imogen tapped the edge of the bridge with her walking stick. The crack of wood on stone sounded solid enough, and she took one cautious step onto the deck, praying fervently she wasn't about to step out into clear space and a very long fall to her death.

The moment her feet touched the bridge surface, her ears popped, and the vertigo that plagued her a moment earlier struck full force. She staggered sideway, coming up hard against a parapet. Her vision swirled before clearing at the same time her roiling stomach lurched to a merciful stop. An ivy leaf tickled her nose, and she swatted it away.

The bridge hadn't changed—still abandoned, and decrepit, and beautiful despite its flaws. Imogen leaned between two parapets to glimpse the river so far below. Were she not given the Blessed Sight by the pendant—"Blessed, my arse," she muttered sourly—she'd die from the fright of finding herself floating in midair.

The intense vertigo left her sweating, and with a profound sense that, while the bridge hadn't changed, her sense of place—of being—certainly had. Every instinct she possessed sounded an internal warning. There was magery here, old and powerful. She didn't need such obvious visual proof or Niamh's sorcerous talents to feel the almost suffocating weight of enchantment in the air.

The twilight deepened, turning the sky lavender, then indigo as night fell fast. Imogen didn't want to risk losing the bridge if she stayed on this side of it until morning, and she had no intention of camping on the deck. She inhaled a breath, clutched her stick in a white-knuckled grip and strode across the span. The feeling of otherness strengthened as she traversed the deck and was soon accompanied by the certainty that something watched her. Her scalp prickled. She held the walking stick with both hands, turning it from journey aid to weapon.

Only her footsteps echoed back to her ears. No calls of nightbirds or the buzzing chorus of insects broke the silence that swallowed the bridge. Even the wind that almost blasted her off her spot on the rock had died. The ivy strangling the bridge beneath its entwining hold rustled, as if commanded by a different, softer breeze. An unpleasant smell drifted to Imogen's nose: decomposing vegetation and stagnant water.

The statues she'd glimpsed earlier stood sentry as she passed. Her curiosity overrode her fear of the bridge disappearing beneath her feet, and she paused at a few of the carved images that were still whole and unbroken. Men and women were represented, some crowned, others not, their haughty, aristocratic faces captured forever in ageless stone. Imogen wondered if these were long dead rulers of Tineroth, their graven forms set to stand guard over the entrance to a forgotten city.

One statue made her pause. It differed from the others in that its visage had been chipped away, scored and blunted until the features were no longer distinguishable. Violence, not weathering, had obscured the face, as if those who had defaced the statue had left it standing as a message—and a warning.

Drawn by invisible cords, Imogen approached the statue for a closer look. A man by the look of the sculpture, slim but powerful. She smiled at such vanity. "More like a gut from too much roast chicken and good wine. But who would want to be remembered that way, eh?" She winked at the faceless statue.

He loomed above her, raised on a square pedestal like his compatriots. Chiseled inscriptions decorated the base, ancient runes and symbols she couldn't read. She reached out to trace them and just as quickly yanked her hand back as sharp pinpoints of pain penetrated her gloves and snapped against her fingers. Whatever sorcery cloaked this bridge, it didn't want anyone touching the statues.

Still feeling as if she were being watched and afraid she'd committed a major offense, Imogen bowed to the statue. "My apologies," she said and backed away. Niamh's childhood reprimand of "keep your hands to yourself," had far more layers of wisdom to it than safeguarding others from Imogen's curse.

She resumed her journey across the bridge, picking up the pace until she reached the other side. Her relief at stepping on natural earth was short-lived. The luminescent path guiding her way dimmed beneath the fog she'd seen from the other side of the gorge. White tendrils hugged her ankles and slipped over her knees like ghostly hands of a crowd of children. The notion made her shiver, and she pushed the miasma away with Niamh's walking stick.

"Stop that," she admonished, and to her astonishment, the mist obeyed, rolling far enough away so that she could once more see open ground and the brightness of the enchanted road.

Imogen glanced behind her and forgot to breathe. The bridge faded, losing solidity until it was no more substantial than the fog before disappearing altogether. Fear threatened to overwhelm her hard-won calm. She crushed it down. Too late to turn back now. She gripped the walking stick, put her back to the gorge and followed the lit path, traveling deeper into vegetation that was more jungle than forest. The vines smothering the bridge grew here as well, carpeting the understory in a damp mat of tangled strands and leaves turned black with rot.

The trees themselves were far different and infinitely stranger than those across the gorge. Massive trunks and exposed root systems created crevasses the size of small caves, and they dripped a constant stream of moisture in air suddenly warm and saturated with water. Imogen's cloak hung on her in a sodden shroud.

The exhaustion that had kept her fear at bay vanished, and she gritted her teeth to keep them from chattering as she struggled through the dense undergrowth to reach the silhouettes of buildings in the closing distance. The wood's unnatural silence unnerved her. Even at night, forests came alive with evening predators. Those she was familiar with kept away, their instincts naturally warning them away from a human who carried Death under her skin, but she didn't detect even the distant hooting of an owl or see the glow of small eyes from burrowing rodents in the shelter of the great trees.

She finally stumbled into a clearing and exhaled a huge sigh. Here, the air was still humid but not so suffocating. Her gladness at being out of the trees died as she got her first look at Tineroth.

A vast courtyard surrounded by palaces and temples of breathtaking height and grace stretched before her. They were feats of architectural mastery, and Imogen doubted anything built in the Berberi kingdom surpassed them. Berberi, however, wasn't a dead kingdom.

The majesty of Tineroth lay in ruin, its edifices crumbling derelicts of an age only remembered in legend, its very existence doubted by more jaded folk. The slim, delicate spires that had beckoned her from the far side of the gorge were nothing more than hollow relics. Tineroth reminded Imogen of Niamh—a once beautiful woman diminished by an insidious sickness.

"Welcome to Tineroth." Her voice fell flat in the thick air.

There were none to greet her or give her a tour, and for that, Imogen was heartily thankful. Tineroth didn't feel haunted, but that sense of being observed refused to fade, and she eyed her surroundings closely.

The city offered numerous places to shelter, places with a roof and likely a dry floor, but she was hesitant to explore them. Who knew how sound they were? The thought of being buried under a pile of timber and stone that collapsed on her while she slept made her shudder. Death came to everyone, but she didn't want to die here.

She journeyed deeper into the city, suddenly glad for the light that refused to leave her and now circled her feet in a glowing corona. She felt like a walking oil lamp, but it was better than groping her way through the dark with only a weak torch and limited fuel to light her way.

The courtyard led to a line of roofless cloisters, and she followed their outer walls until she reached a much smaller garden surrounded by low-roofed structures that might have been private temples. The windows of each building looked toward the courtyard with an eyeless stare, and she tried not to imagine what might be following her progress from those black recesses.

The garden sported a fountain in the center, dry except for a small, stagnant puddle that gathered in the shallow bowl. A new worry joined an ever growing list in Imogen's mind. She had a good supply of fresh water in the two flasks stored in her sack, but she'd have to be careful not to waste it. She'd seen no clear pools or streams in the dark wood or the city so far.

The fountain was not the only statuary in the garden. Straight paths cut from the same stone that paved the bridge spread like the spokes of a wheel in the garden. They led to a center hub on which sat a catafalque of white marble stained green with lichen.

The effigy of a crowned monarch, also carved of marble, lay supine atop the bier. A Tineroth king, forever bound in stone, rested in eternal state. The light at Imogen's feet cast a golden glow across the marble, and for a moment the stone shimmered in the garden's darkness, illuminating the king's features.

Imogen gasped and took an involuntary step back, signing a protective ward with a gloved hand. The marble visage held an unearthly beauty. Either this king had been blessed with looks that made stars weep with envy, or the sculptor had chiseled the face of a god on a man. No one feature stood out. All came together in perfect synchronicity—finely carved cheekbones, a sharp jaw and long aristocratic nose, a sensual mouth set in sleep. The closed eyes were tilted at the outer corners, and a marble crown bound hair that fell across wide shoulders. These things didn't make her recoil. For all that divine beauty, there was a cruelty as well. If the sculptor had been unduly kind in carving features so exquisite, he'd also been unduly harsh in capturing a malice that ran deep and corrupted the very stone into which it was carved.

She turned away, unable to look any longer at the king's profane beauty. Instead, she focused her gaze on the arcane inscriptions chiseled on the side of the catafalque. Like those of the statue on the bridge, they were written in a language she'd not studied under Niamh and doubted existed any longer outside Tineroth.

"My gods, Mother," she murmured. "What is this cursed place?"

The sudden icy splash of fear against her spine was her only warning of attack before the cold kiss of metal touched her. She froze in a half-crouch, her eyes nearly crossed as she looked down at her warped reflection in the flat of an ax blade. Its razor edge rested steady against her throat, promising a quick and bloody end if she so much as breathed the wrong way.

To her left, a voice—male, soft with an icy humor—spoke. "I think the more important question is: who are you?"

CHAPTER FIVE

Cededa had not expected this—a lone woman wrapped as if she was prepared for burial, striding confidently across the Yinde Bridge to enter Tineroth's boundaries. The mercenaries and thieves who periodically invaded the ancient city to steal her treasures tended to travel in packs as large as sixty but never less than ten and never alone.

He held the blade of his glaive against her graceful throat, noting the familiar markings of a Tineroth key scarred into her neck. Well, well, this was telling.

She didn't answer his question, her gaze locked on his blade, her body bent and still as the effigy she faced. Only the shallow rise and fall of her chest betrayed her terror. Cededa admired her composure in the face of her fear. He eased the blade's sharp edge a fraction away from her skin.

"I'm no longer in the habit of cutting a throat until I've had an answer, so you're safe to speak. Who are you?" he repeated.

Her throat worked in a convulsive swallow. "Imogen," she said in a shaking voice. "I seek the help of the Undying King, Cededa the Fair."

A vague anguish pierced his faded soul at that last title, one he hadn't heard in four thousand years. His hands clenched tighter on the polearm. "Then you seek two different people. Cededa the Fair died even before Tineroth did."

"Cededa the Butcher then."

What power did this woman's words have that they had awakened emotions made dim by the interminable years of immortality? Again, grief sounded a dull cord inside him, followed by the bitterness that had remained a constant companion.

"Ah, well, that's a different matter entirely. Why would you seek the help of someone so named?" She intrigued him, as did her responses.

"Believe me, I've asked myself the same thing since I started this journey." Her voice no longer trembled, and she glanced at him from the corner of her eye. "May I please straighten? This isn't exactly the most comfortable position to ask for help or plead for my life."

Her remark startled a grin from him. Usually his only conversations with visitors to Tineroth were limited to screams of pain and a snarled epitaph of "May your soul rot," from him. This was new, and if he was honest, delightful.

His admiration for her composure grew. He lowered the glaive to his side, confident that whatever trick she might pull to attack or escape him would fail. She straightened and turned to face him. Cededa didn't flinch when her eyes widened before she looked away. He knew what she saw—the living image of the effigy on the bier in all his corrupted glory. Immortality had left its mark, as had the sins of his distant past.

"Why would the name Imogen mean anything to Cededa?" He waited for some outlandish story to spill from her lips.

Her gaze flashed back to him and this time stayed. She was pretty, he observed silently—once one got past the layers of swaddling pretending to be clothes. She didn't possess the great beauty of his long dead wives and concubines, but he would have noticed her had she walked the corridors of his palace—if not for her face then surely for that stately demeanor she wore as naturally as he wore his armor.

Her chin tilted in faint challenge. "My name means nothing, but Niamh of Leids should mean a great deal to the man who owes her a life debt."

Memories cascaded in his mind's eye. Wrenching agony, Tineroth's endless screaming in his head as it called its last living son home, a woman's beautiful face as she bent over him and spoke soothingly while he lay in a soft bed that smelled of sunlight.

"My fair savior with the red hair and witch's eyes. If ever a woman should have been made queen, it was Niamh."

Cededa didn't flatter but spoke truthfully. Niamh had saved him once, not from dying, but from complete, gibbering madness.

"I repay my debts," he said flatly. "But you are not Niamh of Leids."

Again, that lifted chin and a spark of challenge in his visitor's gray eyes. "No, I'm her daughter."

CHAPTER SIX

Imogen couldn't help but gawk. Her attacker was the effigy's living twin, only far more painful to behold. The terrible beauty, trapped in marble, was no artist trick but a true reflection of the man standing before her, his malevolence increased tenfold by a piercing gaze that pinned her in place.

Flaxen hair fell past wide shoulders and framed a stern, pallid face. Clad in an indigo tunic and trousers overlaid by a tarnished chainmail hauberk, pauldrons and vambraces, he was heavily armed and armored. A short sword and hand axe were strapped at his narrow waist, and he casually cradled the hook-back glaive whose blade had lightly kissed her neck. Judging by the manner of his dress, he'd not come to talk but to do battle.

Imogen wanted to bow beneath the weight of his scrutiny. He may not be *her* king, but he was still a king if his resemblance to the effigy was anything to judge by. And not only the king but one possessing the title of The Butcher.

Her back teeth clacked together in a rising chatter as he shifted his stance, and those peculiar eyes narrowed even more. So light a blue they almost faded into the surrounding whites, his eyes reminded her of the blind Blessed—those whose milky gaze saw into the past and the future but never what was before them. Unlike them, Cededa took in the here and now with a predatory gaze. He was as strange and beautifully eerie as the city he guarded. And just as extraordinary. If he'd been human once, he wasn't now.

Had she not watched him as closely as he watched her, she might have missed the brief softening in his features at her mention of Niamh. That softness vanished almost as soon as it appeared, and his mouth stretched into a sneer masquerading as a smile.

One eyebrow rose, and those eyes skimmed her, doubt lurking in the blue ice irises. Imogen knew she fell short in comparison to her mother. Neither tall nor curved in the ways that tempted a man, she didn't possess Niamh's natural vibrancy or sorcerous abilities. Any who met her mother and then her daughter would conclude that the younger was but a weak shadow of the elder.

"Where is your mother now?" he asked.

The grief resting heavy in her heart since Niamh's passing swelled. Imogen blinked away threatening tears. "She died."

The sneer faded, and his stern features gentled. "I've lived a long time and amassed countless regrets. I truly regret your loss. Your mother was an exceptional woman. The world is poorer without her."

Stunned by the unexpected sympathy, Imogen squeaked out a "Thank you." She glanced down at the effigy and then again at the living king. The malice was still there, and the cruelty— stamped into the set of his mouth and the corners of his eyes. She didn't doubt he'd earned his ghastly title, but in that moment Cededa of Tineroth seemed almost human in his obvious admiration of Niamh.

That hint of humanity disappeared and the subtle stiffening in his shoulders revealed a growing impatience. "You have the key I gave her. State your business. I will help you in her name, if I can."

Imogen touched the raised scars on her neck. Though she'd grown used to the warm tingling that remained unabated under her skin, she was eager to exorcise the key from her body. She could find her way back to the bridge and home without it. And she had no desire to seek out Tineroth a second time. She'd manage with her gloves and loneliness. There were worse things than a life of isolation.

"My mother gave me a pendant—silver with snake patterns that sometimes changed. She said you gave it to her as a means to find Tineroth if she needed." She pulled aside the collar of her shirt to expose the length and breadth of the scars. "I made the mistake of putting it on. This is what happened. This and my vision changed."

"You can see a lit path to the city."

"Yes."

"And now that you're here?" His long fingers flexed on the glaive staff. An unnamed fear shot through Imogen. He'd made no untoward movement, nor did his expression change, but a sense of menace permeated the space between them. She knew, instinctively, her answer determined her fate.

She swiped at the scars with agitated fingers. "I want this thing out of me. I've fulfilled its purpose and returned it to its master." She sighed. "I made a mistake by succumbing to vanity, and I'm sorry for it. I just want to go home." The desperation in her plea made her wince, but she didn't look away from Cededa's pale eyes.

He cocked his head to the side, clearly puzzled. "What an odd creature you are."

His remark robbed her of words, and she gaped at him.

He drew closer, smiling faintly when she stepped back to keep the same distance between them. "You might be here to return my key, but Niamh sent you for another reason." His gaze touched on her gloved hands, the layers of protective clothing. "Why are you dressed this way? I've seen people bundled less in the middle of winter. It's spring in your world, yes?"

"Just barely," she muttered. Cededa's lips twitched. The itchy sensation at her neck spread to the rest of her body, and she longed to shed the heavy clothing she wore. In the damp heat, her shift stuck to her like a second skin, and the wool gown and cloak hung on her in sodden rags. She had no doubt if she'd kept the veil down over her face, she would have fainted from the heat by now.

"I always dress this way." She paused, hesitant to reveal what Niamh had religiously pounded into her about keeping secrets—until now. "I am cursed." Curiosity flickered in his gaze at her statement. "Whatever I touch or touches me with bare skin dies. I'm garbed for the protection of any who might cross my path." She laced her fingers together and anchored her gaze to his. "Niamh sent me to you in the hopes you could break this curse."

She took another cautious step back as Cededa went rigid, his fingers clenched so tightly around the glaive staff, the skin of his knuckles looked ready to split. Something ignited in those cold eyes.

Imogen's fearful cry of "Stop!" went unheeded as he dropped the glaive and closed the distance between them.

"Don't touch me!" She struggled in his grip, overwhelmed by his sudden embrace and frightened by the expectation he'd drop lifeless at her feet. He couldn't help her if he was dead, either with the key or her curse.

A cool, bare hand grasped her chin, digging into her cheek to hold her still. He needn't have bothered. Imogen froze, eyes wide as she stared into a colorless gaze blazing with euphoric wonder.

Moments passed with the slowness of days to her shocked senses, and still the king held her, very much alive and obviously immune to her lethal power.

"Why?" he asked softly.

"Why what?" Her mind was mud, too stunned to accept what her eyes showed her.

"Why shouldn't I touch you?"

"Because you'll die." Her thoughts reeled, blotting out reason and even simple intellect. He was alive. His strong, fine-boned hand caressed her jaw, the underside of her chin, her cheek, before coming to rest against her collarbone.

Her heartbeat thundered in her ears, roaring in a rush of blood as great as the river below Tineroth's ensorcelled bridge. This king, ancient and nearly forgotten, touched her skin to skin, and that heated contact was both agony and ecstasy. Her knees almost buckled as he explored the patterns of the Tineroth key welted under her flesh with a callused palm. Deprived of another's unadorned touch all her life, Imogen drowned in the pleasure of his caress.

"Sweet poison," he said in a reverent voice. "I am dying. Merciful gods be thanked. After four thousand relentless years, I am dying."

CHAPTER SEVEN

"No one here, Doyen." The soldier bowed before Dradus, his gaze on his boots.

Dradus growled under his breath, his anger bubbling to the surface. "Someone tell me how a young woman with no magic and no woodsman's skills managed to walk into the forest and disappear without any one of you imbeciles noticing?"

The two scouts tasked with keeping an eye on the witch's hovel hunched away from his wrath and said nothing.

Dradus slashed his riding crop down on the shoulder of the scout closest to him. The man flinched away with a gasp and clutched his injured arm. "Well?" the mage said. "I'm waiting."

The unharmed scout stepped farther out of striking range before answering. "She must have left when we were in the village," he mumbled.

Were he not so disliked by Hayden's army and the general populace of Castagher, Dradus would cheerfully turn both men into torches with a few carefully recited spells. Such an action, however, guaranteed he'd never make it back to the city alive. This troop was loyal to its king, not him. Any unfortunate accident might happen on the return journey. The soldiers assigned to help him find the witch and Varn's daughter would offer platitudes of false regret and swear each other to silence over their roles in his demise.

He clamped down on his wrath and spoke between clenched teeth. "You were supposed to keep an eye on them and their house, not running your hands up an ale wench's skirts in the nearby town." The soldier who offered up an explanation opened his mouth again. Dradus raised the crop in warning. "Don't bother, unless you want a taste of what I delivered to your companion. You said the witch is dead. Buried or burned?"

"Buried. Not far from here, beneath a big tree. It's easy to spot. Whoever buried her made sure animals couldn't dig her up."

"Well we can. Take me there." Dradus grinned as both scouts blanched. "Pray her spirit won't hold it against you when you bare her bones to daylight."

He left the remainder of the troop to ransack the hovel, inviting them to take whatever caught their fancy. The two scouts gazed longingly at the door where soldiers dragged out bedding, meager furniture, pottery and bits of clothing.

"You've forfeited the right to the loot," Dradus said. "Get moving."

Judging by the look of the cottage, there was little worth taking. He'd already scoured the few books the witch kept on a shelf near her keeping cupboard. They contained nothing of value for an adept of his skill, and his disappointment left him short-tempered. Niamh of Leids had once been a magic user of renown before she disappeared, and Dradus had hoped to find at least one grimoire of powerful spells he could learn and add to his repertoire. Recipes for herbal brews and incantations to counteract toe fungus were useless to him.

The two scouts waited for him near the grave site, a mound of rocks placed beneath the shade of a giant fir. A withered bunch of daffodils offered a splash of color and proof that someone had visited the grave days earlier to pay their respects. Most likely Varn's daughter, who had vanished into thin air.

He paused for a moment, brought up short by the faintest touch of sorcery unlike any he'd ever encountered. The sensation hummed along his nerves in fits and starts, fickle as a firefly's light. Just as his senses grasped its essence, it winked out only to tease him a moment later.

"Do you feel that?" he asked the two men with him. They glanced at each other and back at him before shaking their heads. "Of course not," he said. "Why would you?" Doltish louts, the lot of them. They wouldn't recognize magic if someone dumped a bucket of the stuff on their heads.

"Start digging," he commanded. "I want to put a few leagues in before the sun goes down."

"What do you want us to do once we open the grave?" The unfortunate recipient of the kiss from Dradus's crop looked ready to bolt for the trees. Superstitions regarding the dead and their vengeance ran strong in most people, and this scout was no exception.

Dradus spotted a log nearby that made an adequate seat and settled onto it. He smiled at the two men, the smile widening as they paled. "Once you open the grave, I want you to get out of the way so Dame Niamh and I can have a little chat."

CHAPTER EIGHT

He held her chin with a callused palm, no doubt toughened by fighting if his current dress and ease with weaponry was anything to go by. But the miracle of that first rough caress bewitched her. For the very first time in her memory, someone had touched her and lived to tell the tale.

Oh, she'd held Niamh's hand through her gloves and embraced her amidst layers of protective clothing, but it wasn't the same. Her wonder at that initial contact had been reflected in Cededa's sublime features, in his awestruck declaration of dying.

They stood in that half embrace for several moments before he released her and put space between them. That white-washed stare consumed her, turning her knees to water. A sudden thought had sent a new fear jittering down her spine.

"I swear, I'm not lying." She raised her gloved hands. "Were you a normal..." she flinched and corrected herself. "Were you any other man, you'd be dead."

His mouth curved, and the fine lines at the corners of his eyes deepened. "I believe you."

Her shoulders slumped in relief. "Thank the gods," she said and exhaled a stuttering breath. "I really don't want you to kill me."

His soft laughter, free of the harsh bitterness she'd heard earlier, washed over her, as beguiling and seductive as his touch.

"I doubt that me killing you is Niamh's idea of repaying the debt I owe her."

Imogen smiled at his teasing. "No, I'm sure it isn't." She abandoned the smile for a frown. "I didn't really believe her when she said you could break my curse. I only came so you could remove the key. Is it possible you can help me?"

"The key is a small matter. It's my magic that put it there. I can remove it just as easily. Your curse, however, is something different. I've never seen the like, and in my lifetime that's saying something."

He reached out to touch her once more. Again, she backed away, and he lowered his arm. "Forgive me," she said. "I am unused to another's touch."

He shrugged, his bland expression saying he took no insult from her retreat. "I have an idea how to lift a death touch, but it will take time, and you'll have to stay with me in Tineroth until the summer solstice."

Imogen chewed her lower lip. She hadn't expected this. Caution and disappointment warred with longing. She'd come with only the thought of Cededa removing the key. He offered her a glimmer of hope for a normal life. But that hope came with a price and a measure of trust in a fabled king who ruled a dead city.

Surrounded by an unnatural hush and decrepit palaces and shrines etched in moonlight, she wondered how difficult it might be to live within the confines of Tineroth's decaying beauty. She looked to Cededa. His face revealed nothing of his thoughts. "How would I live? I've not seen nor heard any animals to hunt or fresh water to drink. My water supply is only enough to last another day."

"There's plenty of fresh water in Tineroth. I'll show you where it can be found, and the wild life of the surrounding woods thrives. There's more than enough to feed one small woman. You just have to know where to hunt. And there are those unseen who still serve me and this city."

That last enigmatic statement didn't ease her worry. Solstice was a good four months off, but what did she have to return to? Niamh's frail body rested within the earth she loved. The cottage stood empty, no longer a home but a shell containing memories that made Imogen's throat tighten with tears. Nothing and no one demanded her immediate presence, no home or family anxiously awaited her return.

"I'll stay until the solstice." A subtle shift in Cededa's expression revealed his satisfaction at her answer. "However," and she raised her chin, "I don't have the means to repay your hospitality."

His deep chuckle puzzled her. "Believe me, girl. If this works as I hope, you will have repaid me in wealth beyond price. The debt I owe Niamh will be nothing compared to the one I will owe her daughter."

She didn't get a chance to question his odd remarks. He bade her follow him through the city to the royal palace or what was left of it. They traveled along narrow streets lit by a hunter's moon and silent as crypts. Eyeless windows allowed glimpses into buildings swelling with a stygian darkness. Only the silver-gilt streets and the pale corona of light at Imogen's feet kept them from being swallowed by deep night. Cededa's fair hair shone like a beacon as she followed him deeper into the city's heart.

Tineroth was a vast maze of avenues and courtyards, crumbling buildings and abandoned temples. After walking for nearly an hour, they came upon a high wall of smooth stone, cut so perfectly and stacked so tightly, Imogen didn't think a sliver of human hair would fit through the spaces between the stones. They passed beneath an arch that led into another of the courtyards. Here a procession of statues encircled the yard, copies of those she'd passed on the bridge. Behind them, a broken palace rose, its roof topped by a coronet of spires, hints of their once graceful lines degraded by time and decay to jagged teeth that pierced the sky.

Sadness engulfed her at the sight. What had Tineroth been like in its glory? She imagined it in daylight, the grand structures whole and new, people moving to and fro on her now deserted streets. Imogen had lived a life of isolation with only a rare visit or two to the nearby townships. The crush of people on market day had made her break out in a sweat every time, but she'd been enamored by the life and bustle around her, so different from the quiet solitude of the cottage. How fantastic must this city have been so long ago.

A pair of iron gates, cast in a delicate filigree design that reminded Imogen of the enchanted pendant, hung skewed on twisted hinges. A gap between them allowed her and Cededa to pass through easily into the palace's interior. Inside, a syrupy blackness snuffed out all light, including the pool of radiance beneath her. That prickling feeling of being watched intensified.

"Sire?" Her softly spoken call boomed in the suffocating stillness. She yelped at the sudden ghostly touch on her arm.

"Peace, Imogen. I'm here."

As if his words broke a sleeping spell, flames erupted from torches lining lime-washed walls. The light beat back a hovering gloom to reveal a vast presentation chamber fallen to disuse. Dust blanketed every surface in a thick shroud. Tables and chairs lay overturned and scattered throughout the hall, as if a great brawl had erupted and the fighters used the furniture as weaponry. A grand throne, perched atop a pyramid of narrow stairs resided over the ruin. High above, the swoop of an arched ceiling, buttressed by massive wood beams, flickered and faded in the dance of shadows. Where the glass of tall windows once filtered light, only open sills remained, revealing the drift of gray clouds across the night sky.

"This was your home?"

"It is still my home."

Imogen winced. Damn her and her careless tongue! She wasn't used to conversing with others besides Niamh, and it showed. She bowed. "I meant no offense."

"None taken." He touched her arm again, and this time she didn't automatically jerk away. "Follow me. There's a chamber upstairs you can use while you're here."

He led her through the hall and up a spiral of stairs to a long gallery still roofed. Faded murals of landscapes and people decorated the walls. Torches flared to life as they passed, lit by unseen hands, and Imogen wondered how easy it was to get lost in the king's palace. They finally stopped before a set of ornately carved doors that opened silently at Cededa's touch.

More torches lit, and Imogen gasped at the neglected splendor before her. Murals and chipped gilt decorated the walls and wood molding. Scenes of palace life captured the eye, chief among them scenes of a wedding between a royal bride and a Tineroth king, a grand marriage of state attended by thousands. Time had not been kind to the mural, nor had the human hand. The king's face had been obliterated by the harsh battering of a chisel. The queen's features, still lovely despite the faded paint, remained untouched.

A large bed, its frame rotted and collapsed on one side stood against the far wall. The mattress had disintegrated, chewed away by nesting mice. A single chair, still intact, occupied space near the cold hearth. The musty smell blanketing the chamber lightened with the cooling breeze drifting in from two broken windows.

Imogen didn't care about the neglect. She'd been prepared to sleep outside on the ground. Now, she had shelter—a roof over her head and some measure of protection from the elements. As it was, she was so tired from her journey and the shock of actually finding the Undying King, she'd happily sleep on the floor, wrapped in her cloak.

Cededa gestured toward the chair. "Make yourself comfortable. I'll return with fresh water to drink and more to wash off the road dirt." He looked to the pack tied to her back. "Do you still have rations? If not, I can hunt."

She leaned her walking stick against one wall and shrugged the pack off drooping shoulders. Exhaustion set in, and she squinted at Cededa with blurry eyes. Sleep, more than hunger, called to her now. "I have enough for two more days, thank you, but the wash water would be most welcome."

He left her to get comfortable, promising to return with the water. Imogen used the brief solitude to explore the solar. She eyed the mural that ran from one corner of the room to the other.

A great wedding. An elegant bride. A crowned king with long blond hair and a ruined face, his pride and hauteur evident in his erect carriage, even in the flat rendition of his likeness on the limed wall.

She drew closer to the mural. Her fingers traced light patterns over the scarred stone where the king's face had once been painted. Like the statue on the bridge, this had been purposefully defaced and with such violence she shivered and pulled away. The chair by the hearth beckoned, and she sank into it, relieved the fragile wood held under her weight. Her feet throbbed, and her back hurt. Teased by the air drifting in from the window, she picked at her heavy clothing before shedding the cloak, hat and gloves. Her skirts and shift still stuck to her, but at least the draft cooled her hot skin.

She leaned her head back against the chair's top rail and waited for Cededa. Exhaustion settled in. Days of travel and sleepless nights spent outside in the cold had taken their toll. The chair felt wondrous, as luxurious as a plump mattress. She settled deeper into the seat and closed her eyes. Just a moment or two. That's all she needed; then she would explore the room more thoroughly. Just a moment...

CHAPTER NINE

Still reeling inwardly at his first taste of mortality in more than a hundred lifetimes, Cededa leaned against the door frame and watched his guest slumber. Darkness, thick as blood and headier than poison-laced mead had rushed through him in a black wave when he pressed his fingers to Imogen's smooth skin. The sensation had almost brought him to his knees.

He'd lost count of the times he prayed for death. But gods long vanished didn't hear his entreaties; the vengeful ghosts who kept company with him in the silent city did, and their spectral mockery held no mercy. Yet something heard—and answered. The proof sat slumped in a chair, snoring softly, unaware of his scrutiny.

Her curse offered him the hope of salvation, of a true and everlasting sleep, where Tineroth's constant voice would be forever silenced and the Living Waters finally ran dry in his veins. The prideful part of him wanted to assure her he could indeed rid her of her burden and the burden of his own immortality. He was, after all, the Undying King. A mage, a great warrior. Powerful. Eternal. Instead, he'd offered a sliver of hope—the "might" in his answer and a time frame of four months. If he couldn't break the curse by then, he'd admit defeat and send her home before the city once again vanished between time and worlds, his debt to Niamh still outstanding.

Cededa's hard gaze swept the chamber. His second consort's solar must seem grand beyond imagining to a village girl raised in solitude by her hedgewitch mother. He'd followed the path of her wide-eyed admiration, remembering the chamber as it once was when Helena held court here, her beauty the stuff of song and legend.

She'd been his favorite wife, and he had loved her as much as his shriveled, avaricious heart allowed. It hadn't been enough. He turned away from the mural, refusing to think on a wife now no more than dust.

The sinuous mist greeting Imogen at the bridge curled around his ankles, caressing his calves and knees. It had followed him into the chamber, spreading across the floor until it flooded the space in a shallow sea.

"Make it livable for our guest," he ordered, and the mist obeyed. Vaporous bindweeds slithered across the bed, sparking spectral lights of indigo and green as they curled over split wood. In their wake, the wood gleamed, as if newly made and polished. Where only broken slats once lay in disarray, a plump feather tick filled the middle space, complete with silk pillows and bedding woven of finely spun thread. Curtains hung from the canopy, and nearby a table bearing a pitcher and basin brimming with water appeared, followed by a stack of drying cloths and a goblet.

The mist gathered itself and slid along the walls as if to repair the faded murals. "Leave it." Cededa's sharp command halted its movements before it rolled back toward the door.

Imogen didn't stir at his voice. Cededa trod on silent feet until he stood directly in front of her. Death's handmaiden was a girl of banal looks—pretty but not extraordinarily so. She didn't compare to Helena or even the vibrant Niamh. Still, he admired her smooth skin and long plait of dark hair with its hints of red. She'd removed her gloves, and he caught his breath.

She had stunning hands. Finely sculpted fingers and narrow palms, they rested limply in her lap, reminding him strangely of swans. Those delicate hands carried an atavistic, malignant power that quite possibly held the key to his freedom.

He murmured a quiet spell. She sank further into the chair, her breathing deepening. Drawn by the promise of her darkness surging through him once more, he circled her slender neck with his fingers and traced the pattern of scars that stretched across her collarbones. As if awakened by his touch, the raised pattern bled out from under her skin, curling around his fingers in ashen wisps that solidified into silver tendrils. They writhed across his hand, gathering in his palm until he once again held the pendant he'd given to Niamh almost thirty years earlier.

The silver glinted in the torchlight as he lifted the chain and slipped it over his head. He sighed as it sank into his chest, marking the skin in glowing etchings that spread from shoulder to shoulder and partway up his throat, twin to those tattooed on the back of his right hand. A jolt of lightning shot through him, and he stiffened. His nostrils flared at the renewal of senses he'd thought long dead—desire, smell, taste—all the things mortal men took for granted, and ones he thought never to feel again. His thoughts whirled, and he touched his chest where the pendant had disappeared. Imogen and her curse. The pendant was tainted with it, and once more Cededa tasted the intoxicating elixir of mortality.

He stared at his unexpected guest, slumbering so innocently in his dead wife's solar. "We will consume each other, girl. I think it's inevitable."

CHAPTER TEN

Imogen awoke to a chamber vastly transformed from the night before. She no longer slumped in the chair but lay across a soft mattress, covered in an embroidered blanket. Somewhere, between the chair and the bed, she'd lost her clothes except for her shift, and the feel of fine linen and silk on her skin made her sigh and loll deeper in the bed for a moment.

Cededa must have carried her from the chair to the bed. She frowned. The idea made her uneasy. Despite that first terrifying meeting, when he'd greeted her with a blade against her throat, he'd been hospitable. Still, he unnerved her, and she admonished herself for not being more alert.

Sheer netting enclosed the bed in a gauzy cocoon through which weak morning light filtered. She pushed the netting aside and swung out of bed, stumbling as her shift twisted around her legs.

The chamber's ramshackle state had been replaced by one of pristine luxury. Like the bed, the rest of the furniture appeared new, wood gleaming with a softly polished glow. The fireplace remained unlit, but the inner hearth was freshly swept. She padded to one of the two narrow windows. Still no glass or shutters to cover these, but they didn't need it. The air outside hung warm and damp, stirred briefly by the occasional breeze that swirled into the room.

This room occupied a high spot in the undamaged portion of the palace, and Imogen leaned out one of the windows for a better look at the scenery beyond. Half concealed by mist made jaundiced by a weak sun, the broken city slumbered undisturbed by the voices of people or even bird song.

The oppressive silence that hung over Tineroth permeated the palace as well. Imogen left the window and padded to the door on bare feet. Even the hinges didn't squeak as she opened it and peeked into the hallway. Only shadows greeted her. Wherever Cededa was, she suspected he'd remain unseen until he chose to reveal himself.

Assured of a modicum of privacy, she retreated into the room. Someone had left a pitcher of water and a bowl on a table by the bed. She found a chamber pot tucked under the bed and dry cloths stacked atop a clothes chest. She set to her morning ablutions, stripping off her shift to treat herself to a quick sponge bath.

The first touch on her neck, smooth and unblemished by the pendant scarring, made her cry out and then laugh. The room held no mirror to confirm what her fingers told her, but she sent Cededa a silent call of thanks for taking back his key. He was welcomed to it. She hoped never to see it or its like again in her lifetime.

She dressed in the one spare tunic and skirt packed away in her knapsack. Her journey clothes lay in a pile on the chair where she'd fallen asleep. If she could find a nearby stream, she'd wash them and lay them out to dry, though in this damp, Imogen doubted anything truly dried. Her lips quirked at the thought of asking an ancient mage-king if he knew where the washing bats and lye buckets might be stored.

There was still no sign of Cededa after she'd dressed and eaten from her dwindling supplies of journey food. The city beyond the windows beckoned with all its mysteries and ancient secrets. Who knew when the king might return, and she wished to see Tineroth in the daylight.

The shadows had only marginally lightened when she opened her door a second time and stepped into the hallway. The palace was a maze of cloisters and stairs, and Imogen tried to remember the path they'd taken the previous night that brought her to this chamber.

After three corridors and several blind turns, she was hopelessly lost in the palace's belly. Had she not been raised by Niamh and surrounded by her mother's earth magic, Imogen might have thought it her imagination, but the halls and stairs in this vast place changed their direction each time she made a turn or descended stairs, as if the palace teased her.

She paused in the middle of a long gallery illuminated by gray light that streamed through broken windows on the opposite wall. From where she stood, she glimpsed spires and rooftops spilling over with the ubiquitous vines, a pale sun obscured by clouds.

Hands on her hips, she exhaled a frustrated sigh. "Do you mind?" She called out to the silence. The sudden sensation of another presence—curious and distant, vast—swept across her flesh, leaving chills in its wake. Something listened.

Afraid but determined to find the front door without wandering this unending labyrinth for the next several hours, Imogen held her ground. "I wish only to go outside. To see the city of my childhood fables." She held out both hands, palms up. "No harm intended. No malice planned."

A weighty pause, as if that which observed her considered her for a moment before making a decision. A mist gathered in the darkness of the hallway facing her, rolling across the floor like surf over sand. Imogen clenched her teeth to keep them from chattering and crushed the instinctive urge to run. Niamh's wisdom echoed in her mind.

"You don't run from that which you don't know. Such cowardice elicits bad judgment. Gain your knowledge first. Then decide to stand or flee."

Sentient, purposeful, the vapor roiled toward her, swirling around her feet until it moved onward, pausing at the top of a set of stairs as if waiting for her to follow. She did, keeping a safe distance back. It might look like mist, but it certainly didn't act like it, and if she looked from the corner of her eye instead of directly at the fog, she saw ghostly hands, the faint traces of faces, and the train of a gown in that swirling miasma. Gooseflesh pebbled her arms and back. Revenants. Tineroth was not only ruined, it was haunted.

The path on which it led her seemed straightforward and short, solidifying her suspicions to certainty that the palace itself had been playing a game of cat and mouse with her. She stood before the great double doors in no time. They opened of their own accord, and Imogen blinked in the pool of pallid sunshine that flooded the entrance. Feeling only a little ridiculous, she turned to the mist hovering behind her and bowed. "My thanks."

That same otherworldly curiosity, overlaid with a hint of approval, buffeted her senses once more. The mist rolled back on itself, disappearing into the palace's gloom. The doors closed after it on a dull thud as if urging her kindly not to dawdle on the steps.

Imogen shook her head. What a strange place Tineroth was with its pale, immortal king, and ghostly caretakers. She suspected that by the end of her stay here, she'd learn that the reality of the city far exceeded the fantastic tales told.

Tineroth stood even more derelict in the unforgiving daylight. Houses and temples had fallen to ruin, leaving only the skeletons of arches and broken columns standing as markers of where they once stood. Walls had collapsed, spilling rubble into grand avenues from which flowering weeds sprouted between the paver cracks. The houses and businesses leading off the main thoroughfare into alleyways made the temples look pristine by comparison, their hollow carcasses safe havens only for rodents and the ever encroaching vines.

Her light steps echoed in the silence. Imogen didn't so much mind the quiet as the continuous sense of being observed. She didn't think it was Cededa. He didn't seem the type to lurk once he assessed a threat, and she was no danger to him or those things he protected. Something else watched, a new entity with the same curiosity she sensed while in the palace. The soul of the city itself?

An odd thwapping sound broke the almost sanctified hush, startling her. A repetitive sound punctuated by harsh breathing and several grunts, it was the most noise she'd heard since coming to Tineroth, outside of her initial conversation with its monarch.

She followed it like a beacon, sidestepping piles of rubble and clambering over short walls until she reached a long rectangular field surrounded on three sides by levels of stone seating. In the center, the Undying King exhibited his battle prowess, and Imogen forgot to breathe.

Man-sized effigies made of woven straw littered the field, hewn into pieces. Those that remained standing awaited their fate as Cededa spun and leapt, swinging the long glaive with as much ease as if he wielded a feather. Rivulets of sweat streamed off his bare torso, carving shining lines into alabaster muscle and plastering his pale hair to his shoulders and back. His dark trews stuck to his legs, the damp fabric delineating the long line of thigh and calf. He was moonlight and grace, speed and power. To Imogen, he danced on the air, lighter than a butterfly, faster than a striking viper. The glaive's blade shone in the sun as it sang a metallic song and clove its straw victims into pieces. The thwapping noise had been their dismemberment.

Imogen shuddered and hugged herself. How many intruders into Tineroth had met just such a fate?

Still, she couldn't help but admire his masculine beauty. She was an innocent in body if not necessarily in mind. Niamh didn't believe in keeping her child ignorant of the ways of people, even if she kept her isolated from them. Imogen had often watched the villagers and townspeople those few times she accompanied Niamh to market day, swathed in both concealing cloth and illusion. She'd admired some of the men, idly wondering what kind of husbands they might make. With no hope of ever forming any attachment with a man, she'd kept any longing at bay, forming no infatuation for any she glimpsed.

There were some so handsome as to make any village maid swoon, but none equaled the man standing before her. She dragged her gaze up from a slim waist with muscles tight enough she'd bet she could bounce a coin off them, to a sculpted back and wide shoulders. She didn't have to see his face to be reminded of those exquisite features. He must have broken scores of hearts when he ruled a living city.

A few more breathtaking spins and arcing cuts from the glaive, and Cededa came to a standstill.

"Good morning, Imogen," he said before turning to face her.

CHAPTER ELEVEN

Imogen of Leids hovered near the practice field's entrance, watching him. He'd heard her approach long before she made it to the field and wondered idly how she'd managed to find her way out of the palace. He didn't hold her prisoner, but the spirits that lingered in his home had a wicked sense of humor and a protective streak as strong as his when it came to guarding Tineroth. They would have held her there until his return. What had convinced them to let her go?

A flutter of movement, the swirl of skirts, told him he'd startled her. He walked to one of the enclosure walls to retrieve a cloth and rest the glaive against the stone.

"Good morning, Sire. I hope I'm not intruding."

That cool, measured voice revealed no hint of her surprise, and her composure impressed him once more. He wiped his face on the towel before passing it over his shoulders and chest. He gathered his damp hair into a queue and tied it back with a leather strap. Even now, so early in the morning, the air hung humid and heavy, promising another lethargic day.

The usual numbing dread of dull sameness didn't afflict him this morning. This morning was different. He had a guest, one uninvited but not necessarily unwelcome. For the first time in more years than he cared to count, Cededa felt a measure of eagerness, of excitement. He'd host Death in his abandoned city and welcome her with what little hospitality was available to him.

"No, you're not intruding. I do this each morning. You're welcome to observe if you wish."

He caught the focus of her gaze—directly on his bared chest and stomach. He'd not been named Cededa the Fair as a lark. Before the Waters changed him, women and men alike lauded him as a man blessed with august features. He'd been used to admiring gazes from both sexes, along with many come-hither stares. Imogen wore that same admiring expression, though she wore it for the man who no longer bore a resemblance to the humanity that had deserted him thousands of years earlier. The colorless Undying King had lit the appreciative spark in her eyes. This surprised and beguiled him almost as much as the knowledge of her terrible curse. His eyebrows rose in amusement when she blushed at being caught. Her chin rose and she refused to look away.

"I don't mean to stare," she said in her sure, even tones. "But you are the most beautiful man I've ever beheld."

Her bluntness rocked Cededa. Spoken plainly, with no lascivious undercurrents, her straightforward compliment created ripples across the still pond of his emotions, igniting an already growing fascination.

He'd misjudged her solely on her appearance, so much more subdued than Niamh's. But this regal girl matched her mother in every way. Equal, only different. In his more debauched past, he might have indulged in some flirtatious response. No longer. He'd changed, and her statement was far too dignified in its delivery to deserve a provocative reply. He settled for a quiet "Thank you."

She nodded. "You're welcome, Sire."

He noted her change of clothes—no different from yesterday, except her garb now was dull brown instead of faded black. She'd foregone the hat, but not the gloves. They concealed those magnificent hands, protective armor to shield others from her touch.

Her gaze flashed wariness when he closed the space between them, but unlike the previous night, she didn't give ground. He didn't reach for her, only stood close enough that he heard the hitch in her breathing.

"Do you want to touch me?"

The blush painting her cheekbones a rosy hue deepened and spread to her neck. The proud stare lowered, and her chin dipped. The flutter of her fingers across the folds of her dress revealed her disquiet as she mulled over his request.

The silence stretched between them until Cededa coaxed her to look at him with a finger under her chin. "Do you want to touch me, Imogen?"

She raised her eyes to his. "Yes, I do."

Decision made, she peeled off the gloves and tucked them into a spot at her waist. Cededa drew a quick breath as she raised those fair, deadly hands. Imogen paused. He grasped one hand, shuddering as the remembered black lightning surged up his arm. The sensation intensified as he laid her palm against his chest. "There's no danger to me, Imogen."

She inhaled sharply, and Cededa fancied the heavy drum of her heartbeat vibrated through her palm. Her hand was hot against his skin, the delicate fingertips tracing the silvery patterns now etched along the slope of his shoulder and line of his collarbone. "You're wearing the key," she said.

He was the key. She had simply returned that small part of himself he'd left with her mother years earlier. He said nothing, content to let her explore him as the atavistic power of her curse flowed from her fingers to surge through his bones. Her shoulders shook with a visible shiver, transmitting down to her hand until it too quivered as she explored his torso. She gulped audibly, her eyes growing wider with each passing moment.

Cededa stood as motionless as any of the statues gracing Tineroth, letting her grow used to the notion of touching another. Had he not lived so long in near perfect isolation, the expressions of terror and wonderment that flashed across her features might have puzzled him. Even then, he still had no concept of what this simple moment must be like for a woman who'd never known the pleasure of touching another human being without the armor of her gloves or the fear of killing.

He shivered lightly under her caress, and muscle flexed beneath her palm. Cededa watched her, enthralled by her ever changing expressions—curiosity, fascination, puzzlement—as she continued her study of his body. He stifled a sharp gasp when her palm brushed his nipple. Unlike the cold lightning that razored through his veins from her curse, this touch started a slow burn that radiated out from his chest until it suffused him from head to toe. Desire, an emotion he thought long dead, awakened and bade his body remember.

Despite his best efforts to remain still and silent, he must have made some small sound because Imogen hesitated and glanced at him. He countered her questioning look with a raised eyebrow and a silent bid to continue. She offered a small smile before resuming her exploration. This time both hands journeyed over his torso, mapping the strong column of his throat, the lean line of his waist, the solid musculature of his arms. He was a landscape of toughened terrain, complete with battle scars and fissures that bisected his midriff and ribs. Old wounds that had healed but left their mark and told a story of strife and violence.

Cededa silently willed her to glide her hand across his nipple once more so he might savor for a second time the glowing heat that set his heart to racing. Instead, she did something better, something that had him curling his hands into fists so that he wouldn't crush her to him. She leaned closer, close enough to press her ear against his chest and listen. The soft whisper of warm breath flowed over his sensitized skin, caught the rhythm of his heartbeat and matched pace with it.

Willingly trapped within her embrace, Cededa tilted his head back and closed his eyes to the anemic sun. He was swallowed by a living darkness, a power that strove to bring him low yet did the opposite, awakening him to emotions and sensations long asleep. Death sought a foothold within him, battering the fortress of immortality built by the Living Waters. He clenched his jaw and fought to remain still for Imogen, whose earlier euphoric expressions reflected his own emotions.

Is this what the blind suffer when they can finally see, he wondered. Terror and exultation?

As if she heard his thoughts, Imogen raised her head from his chest and laughed. It was a sound of unadulterated joy. Her eyes blazed in a face flushed with excitement. "I can hear your heart,

Sire. It still beats, even now." Her pale hands continued to stroke him as if he were made of the costliest silks instead of a body that should have turned to dust long before the stars changed their place in the heavens. "You live. I've touched you, yet you live."

Cededa remained silent, letting her darkness surge through him and her hands flutter over him, light as moth wings. He'd give her this moment, this time to bask in the wonder of his unique resistance to her curse. And he'd drink the black tide and pray to dead gods that her fatal touch would somehow release him from his bondage.

CHAPTER TWELVE

Controlled mayhem swirled and eddied around Dradus as the men who accompanied him from Castagher set up camp on the edge of the forest not far from the deep chasm that separated them from the land on the other side.

Dradus sat his horse and stared at the wall of trees across the gorge. They were no different than those at his back, yet something hid in their concealing depths, vague silhouettes that were more than the slant of the sun through the trees. The odd hum that had flickered across his senses when he stood at Niamh's grave sang a continuous melody in his head now, a tuneless canting without words that had grown stronger the closer he got to the gorge.

The girl remained out of reach. His scouts should have easily tracked her, following signs such as footprints, broken branches and crushed leaves. Nothing. There was nothing to mark her passage through the forest. She might as well have been a ghost.

She wasn't, and it had taken the words of one to guide him here. The men who dug up Niamh's grave fled the moment they shoveled away the last pile of dirt to reveal the blanket-wrapped body. The reek of decay made Dradus's stomach heave but didn't deter him from his task. Dark spells muttered in fading daylight dropped the air's temperature from chilly to frigid. His breath steamed from his mouth in wispy clouds as he spoke the words that made Niamh's body sit up, stand and shake off the blanket.

The horror that faced him made him stutter the words for a moment, but he completed the incantation and asked the all-important question. "Where is the daughter of Varn of Berberi and Selene of Castagher?"

Silence reigned long enough for Dradus to fear the spell hadn't worked. He could hardly look at the rotting wreck of Niamh's body as it stood just below him in the grave's shallow pit. Her mouth didn't move, but a woman's voice finally answered him in dull tones.

"Where you can't reach her, mage."

Dradus scowled. He'd phrased his question carefully, or so he thought. Ghosts, like the fae, were bound to tell the truth, but sometimes their truth omitted important information. "Tell me her name and where she is at this moment."

"Her name is Imogen, and she stands before the king of Tineroth."

His eyes widened before narrowing to annoyed slits. "You cannot lie, spirit."

"I do not lie."

Tineroth and her last king were nothing more than fable. A favorite tale told by mothers to children and bards to villagers and townsmen, everyone had grown up with the story of old King Cededa, corrupted by immortality and doomed to imprisonment in a city caught between worlds. Dradus had been fascinated by the story as a child. He had no time for fairytales now.

He recited another spell, this one a geas of truth. "Tineroth isn't real. Where is Imogen now?"

Niamh's decaying, broken body shuddered a moment but remained upright. "Tineroth is real," she insisted. "Imogen stands before its king."

Dradus stroked his chin as a pulse of excitement shot through him. Maybe, just maybe the ghost told the truth. His eagerness to find Varn's daughter trebled, spurred on by the possibilities of discovering the lost city. And all the treasures hidden within her. "Who is Tineroth's king?"

"Cededa the Fair."

He fired off several questions after that, no longer bothered by the reek emanating from the grave or the sharp scent of smoke filling his nostrils as the soldiers set fire to Niamh's hovel. By the time he extracted the information he wanted from her revenant, Dradus had to bite his lip bloody to keep back the howl of triumph welling in his throat.

He reversed his spells and Niamh's body crumpled in a heap in its resting place. The stench intensified, and he backed away to whistle for his makeshift gravediggers to return. They approached reluctantly, covering their mouths and noses with their hands. "Rebury her," he ordered. "And do it right. I may have need of her bones later and don't want some scavenger spreading them through half the woods."

Their muttered curses fell on deaf ears as Dradus strode back to the clearing where fire consumed the last bits of the witch's house, sending black plumes of smoke into the sky. Caught in visions of wealth untold, he hardly noticed. He'd return Varn's daughter to Hayden, humbly accept the monarch's gratitude and promptly disappear with treasure to make Hayden look like a pauper by comparison. This fool's endeavor had suddenly turned in the right direction.

The troop's captain approached him. "Nothing much to loot and no girl to be found. What do you wish to do?"

Dradus smiled. "Mount up. Thanks to a dead woman, I know where she is."

Frustration blunted his initial giddiness now. Niamh's answers to his questions had gotten him this far but no further. He had ridden to the cliff's edge, expecting to find a lost city rising up from the landscape, an easy ride to its gates, an easy conquest once he and his men stormed through them. He hadn't expected a wind-blasted gorge or an endless forest undisturbed by a village much less a city.

Another man might accept defeat, but Dradus hadn't risen to the status he occupied by giving up so easily. Somewhere, on the other side of the gorge, Tineroth hid in plain sight. He was certain of it, felt it in his bones, heard it in the strange, wordless cant filling his ears.

He turned his horse away from the edge and back toward the newly erected camp. Nothing stayed hidden forever. He would find Tineroth and the girl who hid there. He had time.

CHAPTER THIRTEEN

Imogen stared up at the remaining two spires of a tumbled-down temple. Ivy dripped from their roofs in lacy curtains, creeping toward the flat table of an altar open to the sky. "Tell me of this temple. What god did you build it for, and did you worship him yourself?"

"Not a god," Cededa said beside her. "A goddess. And no, I didn't worship her. I worshipped no one, except myself on occasion." His amused look held more than a touch of self-mockery. "I don't even remember her name. A deity of spring maybe, or fruit trees. I recall her supplicants offering pomegranates."

"And you weren't a supplicant."

"Hardly."

In the three weeks since her arrival in Tineroth, Imogen occupied her time with exploring the fabled city and killing its king with her touch. He stood at the top of the temple steps with her, looking none the worse for her fatal caresses. Dressed in worn silk that had once been finer than any ell of cloth she'd ever seen, he surveyed the fallen worship house with a bored expression.

She didn't truly believe he could lift her curse, but she couldn't discount what she saw. What she felt. Cededa had touched her face with a bare hand and didn't drop dead at her feet. That alone had stunned her almost speechless. And she had touched him many times since then at his invitation. He might not possess the ability to break the curse, but his resistance to it left her almost as euphoric as he when he discovered the nature of her malediction, though his joy was a macabre thing. Never had she met anyone so thrilled at the idea of dying.

He was a mystery. Sublime, beguiling, malevolent. Cededa had been a model host to his unexpected guest, but Niamh's words were never far from her thoughts.

"His people called him Cededa the Fair, then Cededa the Butcher."

Even without those disturbing words, she recalled the effigy on the catafalque, the cruelty captured in marble, untouched by time or weathering. He stole her breath, and not just because of his physical beauty.

Cededa motioned her to follow him, and they picked their way through the cascade of rubble spilling across the temple floor. "The father of one of my wives designed this temple," he said. "This one and several others throughout the city. I'll take you to see them, if you wish. One is still mostly intact."

Imogen's pulse raced as it always did now when Cededa offered to escort her through Tineroth, describing the city as it had once been—a thriving metropolis bursting with life and noise. Raised on Niamh's colorful tales of her time in Berberi, she easily imagined similar scenes in ancient Tineroth. "Oh yes, please. I want to see the entire city before I leave." She paused, caught by his first remark. "One of your wives? How many did you have?"

The idea didn't surprise her so much as intrigue her. Niamh might have kept Imogen isolated from the wide world, but she didn't keep her ignorant. While the kings of Berberi and Castagher married only one woman, there were other monarchs who married several, each occupying a position in the spousal hierarchy.

Cededa's mouth, with its natural sneer, quirked into a brief smile. Imogen instinctively pulled away when he reached for her hand. He waited, palm turned up, until she entwined her fingers with his. "Come," he said. "I'll show you. It's been a long time since I've been a husband to anyone, and stone recalls better than I do the names of those I took to wife."

He led her to the remains of a nave and a lone column, its top third broken off, but still standing. Cededa scrubbed away the layer of lichen from part of its surface to reveal symbols carved into the stone. Imogen recognized the similarity between the writing here and that on the bridge beneath the statues. Fascinating, and for her, unreadable.

Her companion traced one line of script with a fingertip. "A monk was assigned to record the names of the women I married. This is the architect's daughter. All I remember of Elsida was fine skin and a crooked-tooth smile. She was my thirty-seventh wife, I think." He shrugged at Imogen's raised eyebrows. "I've lived a long time and married for many reasons; none for affection." His gaze drifted, as if he looked inward at a memory long buried. "I remember Elsida's father better. A man of vision who saw buildings as living beings. I think he left a small part of his soul in every temple and house he designed or built."

Imogen surveyed the temple's shattered shell and hugged herself. If the gods had any pity, they set free whatever lingering soul thread the architect had woven into his creation when it was destroyed. She hugged herself, chilled even in the city's humid warmth. "What are the other names?" she asked.

Cededa's gaze turned outward once more. He leaned closer and read the names aloud, pausing sometimes with furrowed brow as if trying to recall a long-dead wife's face. His hand rested flat atop one name. "Helena. The most beautiful woman ever born. She bore me seven children." He read more names, and Imogen counted sixty-two wives before he paused at the last name. She took a wary step back as his demeanor transformed, reminding her of their first encounter, when he threatened to cut her throat with his glaive.

His pale blue eyes were cold, and he drew his hand away from the column as if the stone burned. "Gruah. My last wife, my judge, and my punisher."

Caution warred with curiosity. Imogen wanted to know more of this Gruah, but every survival instinct she possessed buzzed a warning that such an idea invited severe consequences. Even if she were fog-brained, she couldn't misinterpret the warning in Cededa's frigid expression.

A tense silence swelled between them before she grasped her courage with both hands and changed the subject. "How many children did you have? Just the seven by Helena?" Hard to believe this icicle of a man with his deathless stare had once been someone's father.

He blinked and met her eyes, as if seeing her for the first time. His features relaxed a little, and Imogen breathed a soft sigh of relief. "With that many wives, not to mention the concubines, I fathered armies of children."

And outlived them all, she thought. How sad. Immortality exacted a heavy price. "Did you have a favorite child?"

The space between his eyebrows knitted into a pair of lines. "At first I did." He shrugged. "I didn't really know most of them. Seventeen raised revolts against me. Six planned my assassination. Two almost succeeded." His lips twitched as she stared at him slack-jawed. "Why so appalled? Rebellion and regicide are bedmates in the game of kingship, witch's daughter, and they usually start with one's siblings or offspring."

Cededa the Butcher. What had he done to earn such a ghastly title? What made his children hate him so much that more than a dozen led rebellions against him and six tried to kill him? Maybe it wasn't him so much as their own greed and thirst for power. Hard to become monarch yourself when your parent didn't age or die of sickness. Still, she didn't truly believe him a harassed innocent, not with such a brutal moniker attached to his name. And he called his last wife his judge and punisher. What did he mean? An icy wash of fear sluiced down her spine.

Her expression must have given away her thoughts. Cededa's faint amusement disappeared. He watched her the same way a hawk watched a mouse hiding in a wheat field. "Afraid, Imogen?" he asked.

His tone was dead, flat. Pride might tempt her to deny it, but no one in their right mind would lie to this man. "Yes."

Something flickered in that piercing gaze. Regret. "It wasn't my intention," he said in a warmer voice.

Imogen's fear faded as quickly as it appeared. "I believe you." She didn't lie about that either.

They stared at each other for a moment. Sixty-three wives, Imogen thought, and each likely struck dumb or terrified at their first sight of him. He certainly left her speechless on numerous occasions since her arrival.

Cededa stepped over a pile of broken masonry, smaller bits crunching under his boot heels. "Come," he said. "Tineroth has a library, or what's left of one, two avenues away." He paused to glance at her over his shoulder. "Unless you want to see something else."

"A library," she breathed out in a reverent voice. If anyone ever built a temple to her, she'd ask them to make it a library. "With many books?" Who cared if she couldn't decipher the languages in which they were written. There was magic in the feel of parchment and ink.

Again that brief smile lifted the corner of his mouth. "Scrolls mostly, but there are some books. I can't vouch for their condition."

As he promised, the library stood two streets away, surrounded by a garden gone wild and choked with weeds and the ubiquitous ivy. Cededa helped her over a swathe of climbing vine, his bare hand warm in hers, his body seemingly unaffected by her touch. While in much better condition than the temple ruin they'd just left, the library showed the marks of destruction like every other building she had so far explored in Tineroth. Half of a staircase led to a second floor and then a third where shelves housed what must have been thousands of scrolls. All inaccessible to her unless Cededa could fly.

He chuckled and shook his head as if he heard her thoughts. "I've a few talents at my disposal. Flight isn't one of them." He gestured to a far corner, tucked under one of the stairwells. "Start there," he said. "The newest scrolls are stored in those niches and won't turn to dust when you disturb them. If you find something that interests you, bring it to me, and I'll translate." He nudged her toward the treasure trove and left her to idly explore another part of the library.

Imogen watched him for a few moments. Had he come here when the library stood whole and undamaged? He had once been a warrior king. That was how legend remembered him, yet she fancied he might have appreciated some of the scholarly pursuits.

The scrolls were predictably undecipherable, and in some cases illegible, their ink faded to ghostly scratches on the parchment. She brought Cededa her first armful of documents to translate. He made a perch of an overturned column top and invited her to sit beside him while he read aloud.

Most were inventories of harvest yields or the results of city court rulings. One made Cededa's eyes flash and his lips thin to a tight line. Imogen glanced from him to the scroll and back again. "What is it?"

"A writ of arrest for the act of treason. My arrest." He flung the scroll across the vast room before crooking his fingers at her. "Give me the next one."

She wordlessly handed him another scroll. Who called for the king's arrest those many centuries earlier? Was it even possible to arrest a monarch then? She didn't think one could do it now.

The rest of the scrolls were more like the first bunch, dry accounts of trade goods and shipping bills, marriage records and births. She gathered the ones piled at her feet to return them to their cubby holes. "Your world then is much like ours now I think."

Cededa snorted softly. "I'm not sure if that's a good thing or a bad one." He tipped his chin toward the opposite side of the room. "Try those over there. You might have better luck and discover something more interesting than who bought flax or a pair of oxen."

His words proved prophetic. The first scroll Imogen extracted from a painted box and unrolled made her eyebrows climb. While the ink might be faded on documents of lading, this scroll retained the vivid hues of both paint and ink.

Pictures illustrated inside decorative frames revealed themselves with the scroll's slow unrolling, and Imogen's eyes rounded with each revelation. Niamh's forthright teachings regarding bed play, even the more intimate details she'd written of her relationship with Varn in her journal, didn't compare to the lascivious scenes painted on the scrolls.

"You've found something that's snared your attention," Cededa called out. "Bring it, and I'll translate."

Imogen glanced at him and let the scroll roll itself closed. "I don't think this one needs translating." She picked her way to him, handed him the scroll and resumed her seat beside him. Her smile widened to a grin at his startled expression.

"They kept these in the library?" His obvious shock made Imogen clap a hand over her mouth to contain her laughter. She cleared her throat and grasped one side of the rods as he unrolled the parchment to its full length.

Each brightly painted square depicted a sexual act—sometimes between a man and a woman, sometimes between a man and a man and sometimes between two women. A few involved several participants. The painter wasn't what she'd call an artist, and she had a more difficult time deciphering whose limbs and appendages belonged to whom. She peered closer at one of the scenes. Was that a goat?

"Look your fill?" Cededa's dry question interrupted her perusal. His pale eyes shone in the gathering gloom. "It's getting dark. We'll return to the palace so you can eat. Bring the scroll with you. You're right, it's self-explanatory."

"What is it? Instructions for lovemaking?"

Cededa stood and relinquished the scroll to her. "Hardly. More like fucking." An odd shiver raised gooseflesh on Imogen's arms at his blunt declaration. "It's a list of services offered at one of Tineroth's brothels. Such things were commonly posted outside the business. Odd to find one stored in the library."

Imogen stared at him and then at the scroll in her hands. Her first glimpse of the painted scenes had elicited surprise and then a tingling warmth that coursed through her body. While she wasn't at all interested in the finer details regarding the goat, she did want a closer look at the others. Their graphic intimacy flustered her and left her with questions Niamh had not answered in her bid to prepare her daughter for adulthood, even a solitary one.

While her curiosity about the scroll raged, Cededa's interest had waned almost instantly. Beyond his initial surprise at finding the document here, he'd exhibited no more reaction to it than to any of the dull ones he first translated for her.

Granted, a man with as many wives and concubines as Cededa once possessed, was probably familiar with the how, why, when and where of every scene in the scroll. And more that weren't painted there. Still, his lack of reaction was something beyond boredom of a thing done many times and reminded her of those moments when he coaxed her to run her hands over his bare torso, trace the silvery outlines of the Tineroth key collaring his throat and shoulders. Then too, he showed no reaction to her touch. Only that first time, when he experienced the power of her malediction, did he show any emotion and that time had nothing of desire about it.

Imogen frowned. She had no misguided notions regarding her looks. She was neither plain nor beautiful. Only unremarkable. Niamh had always praised her, but what loving parent didn't see the beauty in their child? Still, she wondered at Cededa's reserve, the absence of either attraction or revulsion to her touch. His was an almost ascetic demeanor, one that confused her, and if she were honest, put a dent in her vanity.

She rose and tucked the scroll under her arm. Her vanity would have to remain dented. The king of Tineroth had generously offered a means for her to live a normal life. She'd not be ungrateful by being discourteous. There were other questions about him she dare not ask, ones far less trivial than why he didn't react as other men might to the graphic sensuality captured in vibrant paint or the enthralled caresses of a woman cursed with death in her fingers.

"What do you want to know, Imogen?"

So lost in her thoughts, she jumped at his voice, uttered near her ear. Cededa leaned in close, pale features sharp with interest now.

"You startled me," she admonished and offered him a weak smile. It's of no consequence, Sire. Just idle thoughts."

He straightened and crossed his arms. "Unlike many women I've known, Imogen, you dissemble poorly and probably wouldn't recognize coyness if it bit you on the hand." He returned to his seat on the column top. "I've almost nothing left to me except time, and far too much of that. We can sit here all night if you wish until you choose to tell me why you're frowning and burning holes through me with your stare.

She blushed, scrambling for some response that might appease him. "Would you believe me if I said I was admiring your looks?" She groaned under her breath. That was less than inspiring.

Cededa laughed, the expression temporarily ridding his fair features of the malice carved around his mouth. Imogen really did gawk at him with admiration then. He was truly breathtaking to behold.

The laughter died, but a smile remained. "Make no mistake. I'm flattered, but you've complimented me many times on my handsomeness without impaling me with a look."

He'd given her the perfect opening for which to satisfy her curiosity; still, Imogen floundered. How did one ask so intrusive a question without sounding shallow, or even worse, insulting? She grasped another, less controversial topic.

"How is it you speak my language?" She brightened. That was good. And true. Too overwhelmed by Tineroth and its solitary ruler, she hadn't even considered the oddity of his ability to speak her tongue so easily.

His eyes narrowed, his gaze measuring as if he judged her honesty and found it lacking. "Your mother," he said. "She read to me as I healed from wounds. I listened, and I learned."

It was Imogen's turn to give him a doubtful look. That wasn't quite how Niamh described it. Ash and bone coming together to remake an entire man was a lot stranger and more complex than healing wounds.

"I've never seen you eat or drink," she said. "Not in all the time I've been in Tineroth. Do you not hunger or thirst?"

Cededa scowled. "I suspect that isn't the question hovering on your tongue. But I'll answer it." He stood a second time and grasped her hand. "Come with me. I've something to show you."

He led her back to the palace, through hallways and past rooms she'd become familiar with, down stairs she was certain hadn't been there earlier in the day.

They entered a suite of rooms on the second floor through a pair of enormous doors equal to those that served as the palace entrance. Inside, an impenetrable blackness reigned until Cededa conquered it with a whispered word. Torches blazed to life on their own, spilling golden light across a space as grand and as neglected as the receiving hall.

Cededa led her to its center and released her hand. "These were once my chambers."

Imogen pivoted in place, silent and stunned by the grandeur before her. The ceiling curved high above her, beyond the illumination of the torches. The floor lay concealed in a layer of dust ankle deep, but in places where the drafts stirred it clear, she spotted complex mosaics made of brilliantly colored tile. Rotted tapestries hung in tatters from bent hooks, some shredded by age and moths, others by the more ordered cut of a sword blade.

Light flickered on the walls, revealing a series of frescoes that stretched from the floor to as high as the rooftop of her mother's cottage. Those above an arm's stretch were faded but otherwise untouched. Those below, however, bore the same ruin and destruction she'd seen on the statues and the murals in her chamber.

A pile of wood lay heaped in one corner, remains of what had once been an enormous bed. More rubble littered the room, as if someone had come in and smashed every stick of furniture to splinters.

"Gods," she whispered. "Who destroyed so many beautiful things?"

"I did."

Her mouth fell open. Cededa had defaced his own palace? She blinked. "Why?"

His silent footfalls sent clouds of dust swirling upward as he paced the chamber's perimeter. "I didn't do this myself. Men of great anger and great purpose wielded their hammers and their chisels against these chambers, and others, but I was the reason for their actions."

A melancholy settled on her spirit as she viewed the damage wrought. "Is yours the face destroyed on each statue? Each mural?"

"It was my face then."

She shook her head. "I don't understand."

"I was not as you see me now, Imogen. The Waters changed me in more ways than just longevity." He reached out and ran a fingertip over one of the murals, tracing the faded outlines. "To answer your question, I don't thirst or hunger. My body doesn't need food or drink, or even sleep if I wish it. Some might say it's a gift of the Waters to their guardian, a means of survival and protection."

She frowned. "I don't know that I'd call such a thing a gift. You'd never starve, but there is a pleasure in good food, good wine, and a soft bed if you're lucky enough to have them."

His dry chuckle echoed in the expanse. "Yes, there is. And you're wise in your observations. Unfortunately, the Waters' gifts are not truly gifts. Each comes with a price. I have no need of food or water, no need of sleep. My sight and hearing are greater than any mortal man's, and I walk with the tread of a ghost." One hand curled into a fist, though his voice remained even. "But I cannot even eat or drink for pleasure. All is dust in my mouth. I've almost forgotten the sweetness of honey." He paused. "Or the taste of a woman on my tongue."

Imogen stiffened. She'd asked him one question. He'd answered several, including the one she most wanted to ask but didn't know how to approach. "You've lost your desire?"

His short chuff of laughter echoed bitter in the torch-lit chamber. "I lost my manhood long ago. I hardly remembered the belly-burn of desire." That otherworldly gaze rested on her, heavy and no longer cold. "Then you crossed the bridge into Tineroth and brought sweet death with you."

CHAPTER FOURTEEN

Torchlight flickered warm color across Imogen's drab clothing, sparking memories for Cededa of Tineroth noblewomen in their court finery. A glittering procession of butterflies whose jewels caught the light of a thousand candles that illuminated his once majestic throne room. The colorful garb didn't stay on their graceful bodies for long once they reached this chamber, though the jewelry sometimes did.

Imogen traveled the bedchamber's perimeter. "This room alone is three times the size of the cottage I shared with Niamh." Her gaze settled on him for a moment. "Was it yours?"

She shone pale and regal in the flickering light, her dark hair cascading down her back in red-tinted waves. Cededa considered telling her the truth. Before the Waters' effects leached away both his needs and his desires, Cededa the Fair had a reputation known far and wide as a man of lusty appetites and the stamina to match them. His bedchamber had seen many women spend hours in its confines. By the time Tineroth's mages discovered a way to trap and imprison him, it was nothing more than a place where Cededa brooded alone, enraged, impotent, and immortal.

He had lost the carnal appetites that once consumed him only to discover them reawakened by her lethal touch.

The curse flowing black and powerful beneath her skin was killing him and bringing him back to life at the same time. Each day, they engaged in an odd courtship of profound intimacy and innocence, one that left him clawing for control and wondering if his heart would pound out of his chest.

He needed no one to tell him she was untried. Cededa had never cared for virgins. They were too much trouble for his debauched tastes, like high strung horses unbroken to the saddle. Imogen displayed none of those nervous traits, even when she discovered the brothel scroll tucked away in the library. Niamh had done a fine job raising a young woman grounded in practicality. Cededa, however, had no doubt Imogen was innocent in body and unfamiliar with the subtle signals of desire.

Cededa had lost count of the women he'd seduced and who had seduced him before the Waters made a mockery of his humanity. Practiced in the art of sensuality, his wives and concubines had been raised to capture the eye and passions of an emperor. Imogen seduced him with nothing more than her graceful, lethal hands and a steady faith in his ability to break the hold of her curse.

"Sire?"

The single word pulled him out of his musings. He dipped his chin. "My apologies for the inattention. I've something to show you."

He crooked a finger. She crossed the room to stand beside him, listening as he uttered another soft word in a forgotten tongue. The torches brightened, their flames leaping higher to better illuminate the frescoes painted on the whitewashed walls. Not as bright as the illustrations on the scroll, they still glowed, their details highlighted in rich colors painted by a far more skilled artist than the one who painted the scroll.

These were neither landscapes nor portraits, unless one considered scenes of mating configurations of the land. A wide-eyed Imogen abandoned Cededa for the corner of the wall and a closer look at the first painting in the series that bordered the entire room.

Meant to arouse and excite the king and his chosen companion, the frescoes were as graphic in their depiction of sexual acts as the scroll had been.

The first painting showed a man covering a woman, his hips resting within the cradle of her thighs, the curve of his naked flank partially covered by her hand. He lay in profile to the viewer, and bent to suckle the woman's breast. The woman's painted eyes were heavy-lidded with pleasure. Cededa watched, fascinated, as a rosy blush crawled up Imogen's neck and into her cheeks. A reciprocal heat that had nothing to do with Tineroth's warm temperatures, pooled in his stomach before spilling downward. He stood still and enjoyed the once forgotten sensation of an erection.

Imogen moved on to the next painting. Here, the same man knelt behind a different woman, his cock half buried between her buttocks. In the next, the same woman knelt before him, sucking his cock into her mouth. A fourth had them switching places and partners. A different man and woman stretched out along the wall, his face hidden by her bent leg, her expression one of ecstasy as she arched her back and buried her fingers in his hair.

Imogen stepped back for another perspective of the painting, then turned to Cededa. High color washed her cheekbones. Innocent she was but far from immune to the frescoes' effects.

"What is he doing to her?"

He did smile then. "Have you ever pleasured yourself, Imogen?"

She didn't shrink away from the question or avoid his gaze. "Yes," she said simply.

Cededa silently applauded Niamh for not teaching her daughter shame of her own body. Imogen answered him with no more chagrin than if he asked her if she wanted a drink of water.

He closed the distance between them and studied the painting with her. "He is using his tongue in the same way you use your fingers."

Her eyebrows drew together in puzzlement, and she tilted her head as if considering a greater question. "And this is pleasurable for her?"

He gestured at the fresco. "Look at her face. What do you think?"

She bent for a closer look, then turned to gaze at him over her shoulder. "Have you done this?"

This girl didn't possess a speck of coyness. He found it refreshing. "I have."

"Did you enjoy it as well?"

"Very much so."

This was likely the strangest, most fascinating discussion he'd ever had with a woman, or any person for that matter. Imogen delighted him, enchanted him and if he dwelt on it too long, terrified him. Part of him wished he'd met her before his world crumbled around him. The greater part was thankful he hadn't.

She straightened and moved past him, her eyes traveling over the remaining frescoes. All depicted scenes progressively more lurid than the ones before it. "Why did you have these painted in your chambers?"

Cededa had no intention of detailing the debauched atmosphere of his court during his long reign. "They seemed appropriate at the time."

She didn't press him for more but moved on to another question that made him grin. "Have you tried all of these?"

"I have. Several times."

She looked away from him then. Her arms crossed protectively in front of her, and she stood silent for a few moments, pondering, before meeting his eyes. The blush had faded, and her gaze was both resolute and steady. "Once you rid me of this curse, I want to try all of these as well, and I want you to teach me."

She wouldn't have caught him any more off guard than if she'd suddenly stripped naked and ran around the room in circles. No fear, no maidenly embarrassment, only an honest desire to experience the pleasures of the flesh denied to her. Cededa wanted to reply, but she'd knocked the breath out of his lungs, not to mention strengthened the erection that already made his trews uncomfortable.

"What?" she asked when he continued to stare at her in silence. "Do you think it wrong to desire such things?"

The words hung in his throat for a moment, bitter and sharp. "I think you will one day make a fortunate man very happy, Imogen." A brief, agonized jealousy spiked him in the chest, along with the urge to break the lucky bastard in half. He ruthlessly crushed the emotion and tried not to dwell too long on the idea of Imogen as the woman in one of the paintings and himself between her pale thighs. He'd lose the ability to think at all if he did and act on instinct.

She inhaled an audible breath and drew closer to Cededa. A new tension made the air around them almost thrum. Her fingertips grazed the edges of key markings tattooed across his throat and partially revealed by the open edges of his tunic. Her eyes had turned dark, the pupils so large they nearly encompassed her irises. The tip of her tongue glided across her lower lip as she stared at the path her fingers traced. "You are a pleasure to touch," she said in a voice deepened by desire. "A gift beyond price."

The slow poison of her affections inflamed him, and he stood for a moment, docile under her caress as her bane surged through his body, igniting his insides so that the numbness instilled by the Waters burned away entirely. Imogen of Leids was the pinnacle of contradictions – sensual innocence and a death touch that made him feel so alive, he feared he might combust from the euphoric effect.

They strove together toward disparate goals—she to live a normal life, he to die a normal death. They had agreed on a process to attain both. She touched him as often as she pleased, and he bled the curse out of her by taking it into himself. He'd been the one to present the idea, and she readily agreed.

A fine plan except Cededa didn't count on his body awakening so fiercely under an onslaught of sensations long forgotten. Imogen's demand that he teach her the fine art of coupling combined with her forthright honesty in her pleasure at touching him raised his lust to fever pitch. If she didn't leave him be for now, he'd either burst into flame or take her on the filthy floor.

He grasped her wrist and forced her hand to her side before stepping out of reach. Desire, lust, anguish, fear—they surged through him on a relentless wave. This woman had no place with him. He had nothing to offer beyond the lifting of her bane.

"Don't touch me, Imogen," he ordered. "Not here. Not now. Not in this place."

She flinched away and turned her back to him, but not before he caught the shame and hurt stamped on her elegant features.

The tether holding his control in place threatened to snap. He fled, leaving her in his dusty chambers with their lurid frescoes and the ruins of his humanity.

CHAPTER FIFTEEN

For the first time since her arrival at Tineroth, it rained. Unlike the low fog that encased the city each morning and left moisture dripping off the buildings and ivy, this was a true thunderstorm. Lightning flashed to the southwest, and rain fell in sheets, pounding on the palace roof and against the windows.

Most of the time Imogen could predict a storm. Niamh had taught her the old sailor's trick of a morning's red sky heralding a storm, but in Tineroth the sky only changed with the passing of hours, its filtered light dimming with oncoming night.

Imogen stared out the window from her chamber and saw only darkness. Somewhere in the city, or the forest surrounding it, Cededa hid from her. She hid from him as well, still hot with the humiliation of his rejection, the sudden revulsion he had for her touch. He was mercurial as well as cruel, and Imogen thanked the gods he left her alone before the tears poured unheeded down her cheeks.

Now, her face was awash with the fire of humiliation. He had accepted her forthright, albeit clumsy praise of his appearance with an amused equanimity, even complimenting her more than once on her lack of guile or pretense. But sincere flattery was one thing, demanding he play the role of lover and teacher something else entirely. He had turned on her in an instant, warned her off, and put as much distance between them as fast as he could.

Imogen pressed the heels of her hands into her eyes. "You stupid, stupid woman," she admonished herself.

Niamh might have taught her a world of knowledge, but Imogen's bane and quiet life had worked against her, leaving her unskilled at reading another person's subtle cues and body language, especially that of men. And this man in particular.

A new fear clenched a fist around her heart and squeezed. He had rebuffed her, bruising her wrist with the effort. What if he refused to let her touch him ever again? Even if it was strictly to help her break the curse? Panic roared through her at the thought.

Lightning struck close by, blasting the darkness away and illuminating the courtyards and temples nearby in white light. It was gone as quickly as it appeared, followed by a crack of thunder hard enough to make her teeth rattle. Still, it was enough time for Imogen to catch a glimpse of a pale-haired figure striding toward the center courtyard, oblivious to the storm's deluge or its dangerous lightning bolts.

She scrambled for her cloak. She would apologize for any insult cast, any liberty taken. Grovel on her knees if she had to and beg his forgiveness. He'd given her hope in his willingness to break her curse by taking it into himself, where his immortality shielded him from its lethal effects.

"Please, Cededa," she muttered as she yanked on her boots and opened the door. "Please have mercy."

An inner voice mocked her invocation. Why would a man so named The Butcher show mercy to anyone?

Imogen raced into the corridor and snatched one of the lit torches off its brackets. The wavering flame offered the only light to break the sepulchral black of the cloisters beyond her door. If she didn't have that, she might well break her neck falling down one of the ever-changing staircases. She growled when a sudden coldness wrapped around her ankles and tugged as if to coax her back to her room. The palace's spectral caretaker. She'd grown used to its presence, the uncanny way it knew her needs and wants without her ever voicing them. But she had no time for it now. Wading through a roiling chill thicker than porridge, she ignored its mute demand and headed for the nearest staircase.

The stairs faded in the next lightning flash. A hallway appeared in their place. Imogen blew out a frustrated sigh as the vapor swirled around her legs, climbing ever higher. It would shroud her completely if she waited much longer. Desperate and frightened, Imogen stamped her foot.

"Your king," she snapped, "is a coward, and I'm going to tell him so. Right now."

She didn't need Niamh's innate magery to sense the surprise rippling through the mist at her words. It rolled back on itself as if uncertain what to do next.

"Let me pass," she commanded.

A hesitation, then suddenly the hallway reconfigured itself into the former staircase. The mist withdrew, hugging the wall as she descended the stairs. Obviously, no one still in possession of their senses called Cededa a coward, but her outlandish statement had served its purpose by shocking her ethereal guardian into letting her go.

By the time she made it to the main doors, the rain outside had settled to a steady drizzle, the thunder a distant rumble paying court to dancing lightning bolts. Imogen's cloak became a sodden weight on her shoulders. She abandoned it at the foot of the palace steps and sped along the main avenue, hoping she might find Cededa before her guttering torch went dark.

Buildings rose on either side of her, crumbling hulks wearing locks of ivy and streaming rain from broken windows. In her torch's failing light, they resembled crippled giants, sentinels that guarded Tineroth's ancient roads. The vistas branching off the main path captured darkness thicker than honey. If Cededa lurked in those black closes, she'd never find him. Cursing his name and begging him to show himself, Imogen splashed through puddles and yanked on her soaked skirts where they tangled around her legs.

Her torch gave a dying sizzle just as she reached a fork in the grand avenue. The last weak flame winked out, leaving her standing in a darkness so oppressive, she couldn't even see her hand in front of her face.

"Damnation!"

Her bellowed curse shot through the black, echoing back to her. As if on cue, her torch ignited in her hands, brilliant orange flames leaping high. Imogen shouted another epithet and almost dropped the torch.

"You've a surprisingly foul mouth, Imogen."

Cededa watched her from across the avenue, his shadowy form illuminated by dancing flames. Still as the statues of his kinsmen, he sat cross-legged atop a massive altar amidst the ruins of a temple. Rain dripped down his bare shoulders and chest, darkening his hair. The Tineroth key glowed silver across his collar bones and on his hand.

Imogen wiped tendrils of wet hair from her face and prepared herself to grovel.

CHAPTER SIXTEEN

Cededa held back a pained sigh at the image before him. Unlikely as it might be, Imogen had blossomed during her time with him in Tineroth. Where before he'd seen only a pretty but forgettable girl, he now faced a woman as beautiful and elemental as the storm. She marched toward him, her hair a dark silk falling over her shoulders to her waist, features pinched and resolute.

He took the torch she handed him, releasing his hold so that it hung in midair near him. Imogen grasped the hand he offered her and hoisted herself onto the altar stone. She settled next to him and eyed the floating torch.

"Nice trick."

"I find it useful at times."

She adopted his pose, hiking up her skirts until they bunched above her knees so she could cross her legs. Cededa bid a mournful goodbye to the small measure of peace he'd found in the solitary rain and hoped he wouldn't combust on the spot at the sight and nearness of his greatest temptation.

"Why are you sitting in the rain?"

He rested his arms over his knees and laced his fingers together. "Because I haven't felt true rain in a long time." He raised his face to the drizzle, hoping its coolness might lower the rising heat in his veins. "Tineroth sits between worlds, unchanged by time or tide. You've seen the way the sun shines here?" Imogen nodded. "It's the same each day—as it was the day my mages betrayed me and consigned Tineroth to a vanishing exile." He blinked droplets from his lashes so he might see her more clearly. Rain dripped from the ends of her dark hair, cascading in silver rivulets down her neck and between the gentle swell of her breasts exposed above her bodice. "Until the solstice, Tineroth exists partially in your world. Thus, the storm and why I pay it my respects."

How pathetic he'd become. Once the greatest king in all the world, he now sat on a cracked altar stone of a long-forgotten god and sought solace in a mundane rainstorm.

"What do you want, Imogen?" His abrupt question shattered the quiet.

Her pale fingers clenched the folds of her dripping skirt, and she stared at her lap. "I've come to apologize," she said.

Had she told him there were pink dragons fluttering about the forest surrounding the city, he wouldn't have been half so surprised. He stared at her, mulling over what she might have done that required an apology. He stiffened. Had she found the hidden spring from which the Waters bubbled? Horror twisted his gut into a dozen knots. Had she found it and drank from it?

"Apologize for what?" he asked through clenched teeth. Sick with dread, he held his breath while he waited for her answer.

She glanced at him briefly before looking away. Tiny raindrops formed jewels on the tips of her eyelashes before falling to splash on her hands. "I forgot my place. Legend you might be, but you are still a king. I'm a hedgewitch's fosterling."

Cededa scraped a hand over his face, almost lightheaded with relief. He hadn't a clue what she was talking about, but she said nothing of the Waters, and he was very good at detecting lies. Imogen didn't lie.

"I don't understand," he said, pleased his voice wasn't as shaky as his insides felt.

Torchlight revealed her reddening cheeks. "I wanted you to be my teacher, my lover. I overstepped my bounds."

He'd never survive this conversation if she kept kicking him in the gut. He gaped at her. "Is that what you think?"

"You pushed me away and ordered me not to touch you again," she said in a small, warbling voice. "You don't have to be my lover, but please allow my touch. I can't break the curse myself."

Cededa offered up a silent plea for patience to whomever might be listening. He reached out to lightly stroke her wet locks. She shivered at the caress but still refused to look at him. "That isn't quite what I said, Imogen. I told you not to touch me then, in that room, in that moment."

Her brow knitted, and this time she met his gaze with a puzzled one of her own. "There's a difference?"

He chuffed and offered her a faint smile. "Like a pond compared to the sea." He sobered. "Your bane has been my blessing. Those desires once dead for me are alive again. I may be resistant to your curse, but I'm no longer resistant to your touch."

Sparks lit Imogen's eyes, and her back straightened. Meekness forsaken, she glared at him. "No offense, Sire, but that's a damn sorry reason to run. Who'd guess the Undying King of Tineroth to be such a coward?" She yelped when he suddenly lunged and dragged her into his arms.

Fragile shoulders and slender arms, soft breasts he longed to cup and nuzzle. She pushed him toward a madness he'd held at bay for more years than the lives of empires. He might be the coward she accused him of being, but she was reckless beyond description. Cededa counted the rapid pulse beats in her neck, tracked the glistening rivulets of rain coursing down her cheeks like tears while she stared at him with wide gray eyes.

His voice sounded guttural to his ears. "What would you have of me, Imogen? A fuck on a filthy floor? In a room where I once swived my wives, my concubines, even my ministers' wives?" He tugged on her hair, drawing her closer, until her mouth nearly touched his. Her quick breath whispered across his lips. "Be glad I walked away. You're an innocent. Untried and ignorant of those pleasures painted on the walls." He stared at her mouth, plump and glistening with rain. Ripe fruit waiting to be plucked. "I'll wager you've never even been kissed."

And oh gods did he want to. But if he did, he wouldn't stop at a kiss. He wouldn't stop at a hundred kisses unless it was to strip off her clothes and fuck her on a wet altar stone in the rain. Her lids had lowered, and her lips parted at his words. He shook her lightly before pushing her away. "You wouldn't survive me, Imogen. I've bedded more than a few hedgewitches in my past and found the pastime pleasurable, but I've no use for innocents. That includes you."

She cowered away from him as if his insults were hammer blows. He unfolded his legs and slipped off the altar stone, eager to flee a second time. She was right. He was a coward.

Her voice, ragged and breathless, stopped him on the temple steps. "Well, I usually have no use for an immortal warrior king who runs from an unarmed woman, yet here we are."

Cededa turned slowly to face her. Imogen had changed positions. Instead of sitting cross-legged, she'd drawn her knees up to her chest and wrapped her arms around them. Whether for warmth or in defensive reaction to his harsh words, he couldn't guess. While her eyes reflected her pain, her expression was serene. "You insist I know nothing of mating, of lovemaking, as if it's a flaw in my character instead of a gap in my experience." Her chin lifted at a haughty angle, and she stared down her nose at him. "I'm asking you to teach me, Cededa of Tineroth. I'm not asking you to love me."

He stared into her eyes, seeing desire, wariness, and an emotion that made his shriveled heart skip a beat. *Ask me, Imogen. Ask me to love you. I could. You would make it so easy.* The words stayed trapped behind his teeth, a plea thought but left unspoken. He returned to the stone, never breaking his gaze with hers. "Yes," he said simply and held out his hand.

They sped to the palace, Imogen running to keep up with his long strides. Her chamber door cracked against the wall when Cededa threw it open and just as quickly kicked it shut with his foot. He spun Imogen until her back was to him and sliced through her lacings with one quick swipe of the knife he carried at his belt. Bodice and tunic split apart, revealing her long back and the graceful indentation of her spine. Skirt and shift followed, falling to a wet heap at her feet until she stood before him, shivering and gloriously naked.

He resheathed the knife and turned her face him. "Afraid?" he asked, his voice not much more than a growl.

Imogen's eyes, gray as the rain-washed sky, flashed, and her chin rose in tell-tale challenge. "No. Are you?"

Cededa had never turned away from a thrown gauntlet; he didn't plan to start now. He shucked his own garb and shoes faster than he'd rid Imogen of hers and yanked her into his embrace, heedless of the fact they were both still wet from the rain. Her skin was cool against his, roughened in some places by goose flesh.

He closed his eyes, lost to the feel of her under his hands. How long ago had he held a woman in his arms? Savored the feel of supple limbs and soft breasts? What madness had seized him in those shadowy years so long ago that he'd willingly traded this touch of paradise for bleak immortality?

Imogen entwined her arms around his neck and tilted her head back. Her dark hair spilled over his hands where they rested just above her buttocks. Those heavy-lidded eyes challenged him, daring him to walk away a third time.

"I've no patience to be a teacher, Imogen," he warned.

The corners of her mouth curved upward. "But I have patience to learn, and I learn best by doing." Her arms tightened around his neck. "Now kiss me, Sire."

He was powerless to resist. His mouth captured hers, opening her to his tongue. She tasted of rain and heat, her tongue twining with his until he wondered which of them would consume the other. For someone who'd never engaged in such intimacy, she threatened to turn him into a scorch mark on the floor. She groaned into his mouth and sucked his tongue. Shivers wracked his body, and she pulled him ever closer. He hoisted her up, hands sliding beneath her buttocks to brace her against him. Long legs wrapped around his waist and squeezed until he grunted a protest.

She was the first to break the kiss and gasp for air. Eyes glassy and mouth swollen, she buried her hands in his hair. "That isn't kissing," she said between gasps. "That's magic."

He carried her to the bed. Her legs slid down his sides as they fell onto the mattress. Cededa rolled, carrying her with him so that he bore her weight. It was she who initiated the second kiss, as all-consuming as the first. Blood and lust pounded through his veins, ignited by the lethal power of Imogen's frantic hands as they stroked his chest and ribs. Her hips rocked against his until his fingers gripped her bottom to hold her still. The motion pushed him to the edge. If she didn't stop, he'd lose the last, fraying threads of his control and come on her thighs.

This time he ended the kiss with a soft tug on her bottom lip. Imogen stared at him, her lips red and full. Her nostrils flared with every short breath. "Why..."

Cededa reached up and placed a finger against her lips. His own harsh breathing clipped his words. "Patience, Imogen." He smiled. "It seems I'm not the only overeager one."

He rolled her beneath him, wedging one leg between her sleek thighs. He braced himself on his elbows, Imogen's head and shoulders framed by his forearms. Her hair spilled across the pillows, dark against skin made rosy by her passions. Slender hands wandered over his shoulders and down his back, leaving heat trails in their wake. Her bane crashed through his body, his muscles quivering under its onslaught. In Imogen's touch, death was neither cold nor insidious but a candent force that set him alight and freed him from immortality's shackles.

"What are you thinking?" she whispered. She tucked loose strands of his hair behind his ear.

That you are beautiful, and I am dying. He didn't answer her. Instead, he lowered his weight onto her, pressing her into the mattress as his mouth mapped a path from her jaw to her neck to her collarbone and finally to her breast.

Imogen arched her back as Cededa's lips closed over her nipple and suckled. "Oh gods." Her invocation became a litany as he teased one breast and then the other and nuzzled his face into her cleavage. She hooked an ankle behind his thigh and pulled. The motion drove him forward so that his hips rocked hard against the cradle of her pelvis, and she rubbed his cock in a wordless plea.

Her actions inflamed him. He left her breasts and rose to his knees. Imogen's eyes widened when he grasped both her wrists in one hand and stretched her arms above her head. "Do you trust me?" he asked. She stared at him for several heart-stopping moments before nodding. Cededa relaxed his tense shoulders and smiled.

Were he not already on his knees, the sight of Imogen bare and vulnerable under him would have put him there. He'd known and loved many women of stunning beauty, but none compared to the supine grace of Death's handmaiden. He held her wrists captive with one hand and used his free hand to play silent music over her soft flesh.

He started at the hollow of her throat, tracing the memory of the key scar that had once spread from her neck to shoulder, much as his did now. Her delicate collarbones shifted beneath skin as smooth as silk. Her breasts swelled to the curve of his palm, nipples—still damp from his mouth—hardening even more at the light flick of his fingers against their tips. Imogen moaned and squirmed in her captivity.

"Be still, Imogen."

"I can't help it." She clamped her thighs on his hips and squeezed.

"You can, my beauty," he crooned.

His hand drifted over her flat belly, tracing the curve of a rib, the bend of her waist, before settling between her legs to briefly cup her. "Release me, Imogen, and spread your legs."

She obeyed him instantly, her eyes glassy, her breathing shallow. Cededa groaned low in his throat as the musky scent of aroused woman filled his nostrils. How long had it been since such a perfume sent his senses reeling? His mouth watered in anticipation of tasting her.

Imogen gasped, her hips jerking when he traced the inside of her thigh before doing the same to the other. Her gasp became a moan when his fingers delicately spread her and began to rub, stroking swiftly until her hips thrust and pushed, and she alternately begged for him to stop and continue. She almost broke free of his grip when he slid one finger inside her, going deep and easily, aided by the slick wetness of her arousal. Her hips bucked against his hand.

Cededa watched her lovely face, the roll of her eyes as she surrendered to his touch, the parting of her lips as she breathed in short pants. His fingers were slippery as he stroked her, teasing, parting, penetrating.

Gods, but this would be the greatest test of his endurance. The desire to pull her legs over his shoulders and plunge his cock into Imogen's welcoming body nearly overwhelmed him. He hadn't lied when he told her he didn't have a use for virgins. They required the patience he admitted he didn't possess. Even if he did, the girl in his arms was doing a fine job of destroying it in a matter of moments.

Her soft whimpers and the rapid rise and fall of her hips warned him she neared her climax. He stopped, withdrawing his finger slowly, shuddering as her inner muscles tightened in protest.

"What are you doing? Why did you stop?" Imogen's hips rocked forward and back as her fingernails dug half-moon designs into his arms.

"Shh, Imogen." He loomed over her and released her wrists. She instantly draped her arms over his shoulders, burying her hands in his hair. He stared into her eyes as he brought his slick fingers to his mouth, sucking each one slowly to savor her taste. She inhaled sharply, her pupils expanding even more at the sight.

She tasted better than the costliest wine. He ached; ached to slip his tongue inside her, to lick and suck her until she screamed his name to the heavens. He rested an elbow on either side of her head and bent low. Her lips quivered beneath his as she struggled to recapture his mouth in a kiss. He held back, teasing her with just the glide of his tongue across her lower lip.

"This is just the beginning." He pressed light kisses to her temple, her nose, each eyelid, the tip of her chin, the side of her jaw.

She sighed, turning her head so his mouth caressed her neck. He worshipped her as devoutly as any believer before the altar of a forgotten god. Muscle rippled and flexed where his tongue traveled. Cededa returned to her breasts, drawing ever tightening concentric circles with his tongue until he reached her nipples and sucked them into his mouth. Imogen groaned his name and urged him on with her hands cupping his head.

He loved her leisurely, savoring the varying textures of her skin, the flat expanse of her belly and gentle angle of her hipbones. Her thighs splayed wide, beckoning him as he backed toward the foot of the bed. The taste of her on his fingers only swelled his hunger for more. He slid his hands under her buttocks and lifted her to his mouth.

Imogen nearly came off the bed at the first flick of his tongue. Only Cededa's grip on her hips held her there. She chanted his name between moans as he made love to her with his mouth. Her pelvis butted his chin as she pushed against him. His shoulders flexed under the weight of her legs as she dug her heels into his back and bucked in the throes of climax.

Imogen went from rigid to boneless, her legs falling away from his back. Cededa laved the wetness coating her entrance, making her jump. He was a breath away from coming on the sheets. His arms shook as he rose above her. She'd never be more ready for him than now, and he had neither the will nor the control to prolong the moment.

Torchlight flickered over her body, and her chest rose and fell with her staccato pants. The sweep of her hand over his chest and stomach made his aching cock throb even harder. "That was my favorite of the frescoes in your bedchamber," she said with a lazy smile.

Caught between laughter and a groan, he pressed down on her, widening her legs even more to accept his hips and prepare for his possession. She was untried if no longer so innocent. He had eased her tight passage open with his fingers, aided by the natural wetness of her desire, but some discomfort was unavoidable, no matter how much care he took.

Fearless Imogen brushed aside his hesitation by wrapping her legs around his hips, anchoring him to her. "Teach me," she said and punctuated the command by rubbing against his shaft where it nestled between her thighs.

She was neither mage nor witch, but those two words beguiled him, snapping the thin cord of his restraint. Cededa cupped her face in his hands. "Look at me, Imogen."

He stared into her eyes and pushed, the head of his cock stretching muscles swollen by her climax. They closed around his shaft, squeezing. He gasped, the sound echoed by Imogen who stiffened in his arms but didn't look away. Her knees dug into his ribs, her heels into his lower back as he slid slowly inside her.

She clasped him like a well-made glove. Cededa shuddered in her arms, overwhelmed by the urge to thrust hard, feel those internal muscles flex around his cock. A trickle of sweat meandered down Imogen's temple and disappeared in her hair. Cededa kissed the spot, tasting salt. She lay rigid in his arms, her shallow breaths tickling his shoulder. He kissed the curve of her ear, leaving it to feather his lips across her hot cheek to her eyelid.

He rested halfway inside her, nearly mad with the urge to thrust deeper. Instead, he plied more kisses to her face, learning the landscape of her features; no longer banal to him but beautiful. Her body slowly relaxed against his, and Cededa swallowed back a triumphant cry when Imogen's hips tentatively rocked forward, sheathing him a little more.

Her lips were soft under his, her tongue warm as it glided languidly over his bottom lip. He deepened the kiss, filling her mouth with his tongue in the same way his cock filled her body. He pulled away to gaze into her eyes once more. "A little more, Imogen, just a little more. I promise."

He thrust, sliding deep until his bollocks pressed against the curves of her buttocks. Imogen grunted, her eyes wide. She curled upward, sinking her teeth into his shoulder. Cededa groaned low and long, caught between the ecstasy of possession and the sting of her bite blossoming across his shoulder. He tugged on her hair, pulling her head back so he could look at her.

Pain, challenge and desire swirled in her gaze. "Well met, my beauty," he rasped. "Well met."

He kissed her hard, opening her mouth to accept his tongue as he'd opened her body to accept his cock. Imogen's hands tangled in his hair, trapping him, and soon the ravager became the ravaged.

His plans to go slowly, to initiate her gently, went up in flames at the urging of her hips against his. He slid partway out of her only to surge inside once more, hard enough to push her across the bed. He loved her; he fucked her and ultimately possessed her. All while the deadly force of her bane washed through his veins.

He buried his face in Imogen's neck and breathed the perfume of flowers from her hair. Her scent, her taste, the feel of her around him sent him spiraling out of control. He plunged into her, over and over, gripping her hips hard enough to leave marks. On the edge of orgasm, he sucked on the soft skin of her neck and moaned her name in her ear. Sensation drowned him in a tide. Heavy groans spilled from his lips as Imogen rocked against him, milking his cock until his bollocks were empty, and he collapsed on her, utterly spent.

Her "oomph" made him roll away. He took her with him, a hand on her buttocks to maintain their connection.

They remained that way for several moments, embracing but silent. Cededa threaded his fingers through Imogen's hair, relishing the feel of her body against his, the slippery clasp of her inner muscles on his softening cock, as if her body sought to keep him inside her a little longer. Her position and the fall of her hair hid her face from him. Her hand rested lightly on his hip, the other tucked under his hair to rest warmly against his nape. Her breath drafted across his neck, making the Tineroth key vibrate gently under his skin. He wanted to see her expression as she lay in his arms in the aftermath of their lovemaking, but he waited, content to lie beside her and stroke her back.

Imogen finally lifted her head, gifting him with a smile that had him hardening inside her. "I think that takes care of two frescoes." She winked. "You'll teach me the rest, yes?"

Delighted and relieved, Cededa chuckled and pulled her even closer against him. He kissed her softly, coaxing a moan from her to match his. "Aye," he said after a few more drugging kisses. "As long as you're a willing student, I'll teach you everything I know."

Her expression sobered. She ran a finger across his forehead before tracing a line down his nose to the creases that bracketed either side of his mouth. "Thank you," she said. "For a man who had sixty-three wives, what we did might be of small consequence to you, but it was...wondrous to me."

Cededa stared at her, words locked in his throat as emotions either long dead or never felt before threatened to choke him. "It was no less for me, Imogen," he finally said and pressed his cheek to hers. Wondrous indeed. Devastating and bludgeoning. The horror of the shade didn't reside in her hands but in the inevitability of her leaving him. His hand clenched into a fist behind her back before he gathered her even closer.

"Will you teach me more tonight, Cededa?" A soft yawn punctuated her question.

He liked the sound of his name on her tongue. His answering chuckle sounded brittle to his ears. "I think you've had enough for one evening." Her invitation to make love to her again sent another wave of heat coursing through him. If she didn't need time to recover, he'd swive her all night. As it was, he'd have to clamp down on his desires for now.

"You'll stay with me?" she asked and yawned a second time. "Even if you don't sleep?"

He might be immortal and half-mad; he wasn't a fool. Imogen gave a sleepy gasp when Cededa slipped out of her. Her thighs were wet with his seed as were his. A bath tomorrow for them both. The frescoes in his room didn't depict lovemaking in a bath, but he didn't think Imogen would mind him teaching her that particular pleasure.

The nearly forgotten feel of a soft, sleepy woman curled against his side washed over him, as sensual as any lovemaking.

Imogen was already asleep, her slender arm draped across his torso. A faint, purring snore serenaded him, making him smile.

He was more than content to lie here for the rest of the night, listening to his woman's soft breathing and the last of the rain drumming on the roof. Eternity might not seem so long if he had this to look forward to each evening. Imogen muttered in her sleep, and Cededa stroked her hair until she quieted.

He closed his eyes, imagining a life, finite and free of the Waters, where he was mortal once again. Such dreams held their own comfort.

The silence in the chamber deepened, and the Undying King slept.

CHAPTER SEVENTEEN

"It's unnatural to be this beautiful." Imogen paused in admiring Cededa's naked body to give him an apologetic look. "I mean that in the best way of course."

Dressed only in morning light, the king reclined in the bed, leisurely stroking Imogen's hip as she sat facing him. He smiled. "Of course. Considering I'm a few thousand years old, I'd say it's unnatural to be this alive."

She ran a hand over his shoulder and down one muscled arm. "You know what I mean. 'Cededa the Fair' wasn't an exaggeration."

"I was given that title before the Waters changed me, Imogen."

"It still applies."

She caressed his chest, sliding a finger down the line bisecting hard muscle. A myriad of scars, small and large, marked his pale skin.

"How did you get this?" Her palm rested over a puckered round of flesh just below his collarbone.

"Lucky shot from a Partik bowman."

Another scar, half-moon in shape, aligned with his bottom rib. "And this?"

"One of my general's war horses. He kicked me through a fence. I was lucky to walk away with only a few broken ribs."

Imogen winced. "Lucky indeed." She continued her exploration, stopping at a series of slashes that stair stepped his right side. Cuts made by a blade. "These?"

A sharp, indrawn breath made her look up. Cededa's mouth had thinned to a tight line. An old grief flickered through his pale eyes. "My son." He turned his gaze to the ceiling. "Some wounds never heal."

He told her he had sired armies of children. Still, it was difficult to reconcile this legendary, solitary figure with a man who'd been not only a husband but a father as well—one who'd lost his children in ways beyond mortality.

Her heart ached for him. "I'm sorry, Sire."

The shadows in his gaze lightened. "No need, Imogen. It was a very long time ago."

She pushed a strand of flaxen hair away from his cheek. "That doesn't make the hurt any less."

"No, it doesn't."

Imogen shifted positions, bracing her hands on either side of his shoulders. She bent and kissed his scars, touching each ridge and line with the tip of her tongue, learning the taste of him. He'd bear these reminders all his days. She didn't possess the power to erase them, but she could try and lessen the pain each carried for him.

Cededa stretched beneath her, sinuous as a cat. Her tongue teased him, sent shivers dancing across his skin as she licked and nibbled her way from his ribs to his belly. Her fingers followed, dragging across the tips of his nipples, repeating the caress as he moaned and held her waist.

Beguiled by his reactions, Imogen embraced her newfound skills, plying her mouth and tongue across his navel and over the line of blond hair that led to the apex of his thighs.

His cock brushed her cheek as she knelt between his legs. Imogen paused. Last night, she had only glimpses of his nude body, too caught up in a dizzying whirl of sensation, fear and the anticipation of having him inside her to see or fully appreciate him. Now, with the morning upon them and slow time in a soft bed, she could indulge.

He seemed huge in her eyes, though Niamh's straightforward remarks about a man's body had taught her he was likely endowed as other men. Still, the memory of him stretching her, filling her until the pressure in her belly made her squirm, argued he was more blessed than most.

Her hand closed around his shaft. Cededa moaned. Delighted by his response, Imogen tightened her grip and dipped to nuzzle the inside of his thighs, the soft give of his bollocks. His scent filled her lungs, a faint musk mixed with the herbs from the soap he'd used to bathe earlier.

Cededa buried one hand in her hair and reached down with the other to grasp her hand. "Like this," he instructed and guided her into quick strokes. She followed his lead, setting a rapid rhythm up and down his cock that had his hips thrusting in time. His head was arched back into the pillow, lips parted to breathe shallow breaths. His eyes were half closed, the whites showing beneath his lashes.

She grasped him even harder, savoring the feel of the stiff cock slipping back and forth against her palm. A milky bead of semen crested the tip. Imogen slid her hand higher to smear the fluid with her fingers. Incoherent sounds fell from Cededa's lips, guttural, encouraging. She carefully licked one finger, tasting a touch of salt.

A vision of the fresco in the king's chamber, of a woman kneeling before a man, his cock half in her mouth, filled her mind's eye. Flushed and aroused by the feel of Cededa in her hand and the taste of him on her tongue, she bent to suck gently on the slippery head of his cock.

"Ah gods," he breathed.

Hesitant at first and unsure of herself, Imogen soon set to her task, sucking him slowly and then with greater speed, lips curved around his shaft. His bollocks tightened in her hand, and his fingers tangled in her hair.

"Imogen," he gasped. "If you don't stop, I'll come in your mouth."

She paused in her torture of him, remembering the feel of him inside her, the hot stream of seed he pumped into her, the slippery sensation as it dripped down her thighs in thin streams. The memories built a molten pool in her lower belly, and she sucked him harder, deeper. Cededa gasped out her name and succumbed to the sensations overtaking him.

Two hard pulses along the length of his shaft and he filled Imogen's mouth with a thick, salty heat. She swallowed, savoring his taste.

When she rose and slithered up his body, slippery with sweat and flushed, he greeted her with a soft, satiated kiss.

"I'm not so sure you need a teacher, Imogen."

Imogen twirled a silky strand of his hair around her finger and frowned. "Oh no you don't, Sire. You promised." She kissed his chin, the underside of his jaw. "Besides, a man who once had sixty-three wives and a few hundred concubines must have learned a few tricks between the sheets."

She squealed when he suddenly rolled, flipping her onto her back so that he was the one resting on her. His grin set her heart to fluttering in her chest. Gods, he was beautiful.

"A few."

Her eyebrow rose. "A few what? Tricks or concubines?"

His grin widened. "Both."

He ran his fingers down her sides, tickling as she squirmed and laughed and tried to throw him off her. They wrestled in the bed until she was breathless and sweating. Once more she found herself atop Cededa, thighs spread. His pale eyes had gone dark, and his hands gripped her hips.

"Fucking your sweet mouth isn't enough, Imogen. I want more."

The coarse remark sent a flare of heat through her body. She curled her hand around his cock, still hard despite his recent orgasm, and guided it to her entrance, slick and aroused by his nearness and his words. "How much more?" she teased and slid partway down.

The faint soreness lingering from the previous night gave way to a throbbing. She moaned, the sound echoed by Cededa.

He gripped her hips in hard hands and thrust upward, going deep until she'd sheathed his cock completely. "All of you. I want all of you."

Outside the sun rose, its light brightening the chamber as morning warmed to noon and Cededa introduced Imogen to many more pleasures of the flesh.

When they finally left the bed, she was weak-kneed and starved.

"You might not have to eat, but I think I could eat an entire boar by myself."

As if on cue, Cededa's stomach growled. His eyes widened. Were she not as shocked as he by the sound, Imogen might have laughed at the amazed expression on his face.

"When was the last time your belly made that noise?"

He rubbed his midriff. "Kingdoms have risen and fallen since I last ate a meal."

"That's a long time between breakfast and dinner, Sire."

"True." Cededa rubbed the taut muscles and was rewarded with another loud gurgle. They both laughed.

He took her hand and drew her to him. "Get dressed." He glanced at the bag she'd brought with her to Tineroth. "Do you have another shift?" She nodded. "A good thing as I don't think the other can be repaired. Meet me at the library. I'll return there after my hunt. We can eat, and I'll translate some of the Partik tomes for you."

An uneasy frisson skittered down her back, one she couldn't place. There was something here she should know. Some bit of reasoning that was escaping her. "Sire, what does your hunger mean?"

He kissed her and shrugged as if these cravings were nothing more than trivial news. "It means I am awakening, Imogen." He gestured to her bag. "Get dressed," he repeated. "I'll see you in a little while."

They ate while sitting on the floor of the library's vestibule. Dust motes danced in the air above them, reminiscent of the fireflies lighting the city at night. Imogen watched as Cededa picked carefully at the roasted hare he'd provided, slicing off small slivers and eating slowly.

She didn't blame him. Who knew how his body might react to those first bits of food to pass his lips after so long? At his initial bite, she'd prepared to scuttle out of the way in case he sickened. He didn't. Instead, his eyes lit up. "This is good."

"You've a decent cook in your kitchens." She shrugged. "Whoever that might be and wherever your kitchens are."

Cededa laughed. "You're the recipient of the most talented hedgewitch magics, Imogen. Niamh would have approved."

Imogen sighed. "I miss her very much. I'm glad you met her when she was young. The sickness didn't just take her life. It stole her spirit...diminished her."

"I didn't know her that well." His mouth turned up in a faint smile. "Certainly not in the way I've come to know you. What I did know I admired."

She returned the smile. "She was amazing. Thoughtful, loving, sharp as a well-honed blade and educated. I'd never known any to best her in conversation or bargaining."

"Did she ever tell you why you were born cursed?"

Imogen shook her head. "No. She only said she was a coward for not telling me."

He rose abruptly and offered his hand to help her stand. "If you're done, we'll return to the palace. Gather up the scrolls you want to bring with you."

He led her out of the library and across the city's main avenue. They passed the ruin of the temple that preserved the queens' names in stone and crossed the green stretch of the abandoned arena where Cededa practiced with various weaponry each morning. When they neared the catafalque with his effigy, she made him stop.

"Every portrait, every statue, any likeness of you has been defaced. Except this one. Why?"

Cededa stared at his image in stone, his expression so much like the effigy's in that moment, Imogen suffered a touch of revulsion. "It was a message. One carved in marble instead of written on parchment, guaranteed to accompany me into this pathetic existence. There was rebellion in all parts of my empire, including this city. I'd led an army to Mir. While I was gone, the mages and ministers left behind emptied Tineroth and proceeded to destroy every likeness of me, except this one. It was no oversight. No accident. They left me a sepulcher I'd never be fortunate enough to use."

Imogen shivered and hugged herself. "Were you truly so hated?"

Cededa closed his eyes. "I remember those days. Chaos and screaming mobs. Buildings set alight. Temples desecrated. People shouting for the ministers to bring forth the head of the Butcher." He opened his eyes to gaze upon the effigy. "I think 'hated' is too mild a word." He pointed to the inscription carved on the side of the catafalque. "This is written in Scetaq, the language of curses. It says 'Here lies Cededa, alive yet dead. May he remember. May we forget.'"

Imogen gaped at him, unease worming its way through the glow of her fascination for her new lover. "What did you do to turn your people against you?"

"Enough to live four thousand years and still regret it. Still grieve it."

They stood in silence for a moment before he motioned for her to follow him again. This time she didn't take his hand, nor did he offer it. He led her to one of the tall spires still intact and shrouded in a green veil of ivy. Cededa wrenched the warped door open, snapping brittle hinges with his efforts.

He took her hand, and they climbed a stone staircase that spiraled endlessly upward. When they finally stopped, Imogen leaned against the wall and tried not to breathe in great gulps of dusty air.

"What are we doing?" she wheezed on a thin note. She scowled to see Cededa hadn't even broken a sweat from the arduous climb.

He opened another door. Light poured into the stairwell's gloom, along with fresh air. Imogen followed him out onto a balcony and gasped at the sight before her.

Tineroth lay in the afternoon sun, a relic of broken splendor awash in the pale, filtered light of a cloudy sky. From her rooftop view, she saw the green crown of the surrounding forest with its strange trees and hidden occupants. Beyond the woods, the deep crevasse with its ribbon of river.

As if he heard her unspoken question, Cededa spoke. "Once I took back the key, the bridge disappeared. When you return home, I'll summon it again so you can cross."

Despair rose inside her at his words. Imogen tried to brush it away and failed. She should be glad to leave. She'd be free of her bane and could return to a world populated by others, where there was noise and market days and festivals, rainstorms and changes of seasons and the renewed hope of a normal life.

None of that seemed to matter as much at the moment. The king who'd become her savior and her lover wouldn't accompany her into that new life.

"Why did you bring me to your chambers yesterday, Sire?"

He stayed quiet so long, she didn't think he'd answer. "So that one living person might know I was once a man. Flawed and incomplete, but still a man like any other. I bled; I loved; I warred; I married and sired children. I am more than just the Undying King of Tineroth. I am also less.

"When I take you back across the bridge and leave you on the other side, I hope I will leave a woman with a knowledge beyond the stories told, even beyond the intimacy we now share between us."

His words brought tears to her eyes, and she wiped them away. "Why are we here now?"

His measuring gaze held her in place. "You tell me, Imogen."

She looked back over the city, its silent streets and empty courtyards. "So that I might see the beauty that once was." A broken city, abandoned, empty and still regal. "Tineroth is your true wife."

"She is my jailer and my mistress. I am bound to her, body and soul, charged with defending her from all invaders. The cost of the privilege that is immortality."

Imogen turned to Cededa and slid her arms around his neck. He went willingly into her embrace. "I didn't need to see your chambers or even Tineroth from this balcony to understand you or the price you pay. I saw the man within the king, Sire. Even if you had no way of lifting my bane, I'd remain grateful and happy to the end of my days that I met you, Cededa the Fair."

CHAPTER EIGHTEEN

"**D**id you speak much with my mother when she cared for you?"

They sat on the floor of another of the palace's numerous rooms, a low table between them. Torchlight sent shadows cavorting across the walls.

Cededa's fingers hovered over an ornate game piece as he pondered his next move and ignored her attempts at distracting him. He jumped the piece two spaces and removed three of hers from the game board. "No. One of the last things I regained in my healing was the ability to speak. But she spoke to me often enough. Read to me as well. Remember when I said it's how I learned your language?" He moved another piece onto the board, putting her most powerful player at risk.

Imogen hissed and hunched closer to the table for a closer look—a fruitless effort. Nothing hid on the board. He was a master at the game, and while Imogen played well, she was no match.

She studied the pieces. "Niamh wrote in her journal that you were burned."

Cededa waited until she moved her designated piece and sealed her fate in this round of Senet. "I was burned. Burned until I was nothing more than an ash heap and a pile of bones."

Her eyes rounded, horror darkening her irises. "Dear gods. Were you aware the entire time?"

"Yes." He made his next move and conquered one corner of her territory on the board. He didn't elaborate. Such memories were not to be shared or detailed. The agony, the heat, the consuming flames. Jeering faces and laughter, the ribald jokes and toasts with ale cups as he bellowed his pain to the cold moon until he could no longer see or hear. They had scattered his ashes to the winds and tossed his bones into the forest, a desecration of the man who'd decimated their numbers before they overwhelmed him.

He'd lain for days in a pile of leaves somewhere far beyond Tineroth, an abomination half healed, half remade and still smelling of the fires that had burned him to nothing more than scorched bone.

Niamh hadn't fled when she found him. Instead, she'd bound him in layers of magic as natural as he was unnatural and sequestered him a private room in her home so he might renew in peace.

He welcomed the solace, the brief moments of touching the living world, even when the soul of Tineroth and her cursed waters shrieked inside his head for him to return. That compulsion could not be conquered. The city he once ruled had become the city he now served. Once he was whole again, he'd left Niamh's house, leaving behind a key to the city and a promise to offer aid if she ever needed him. He never expected to see her again. He never dreamed he'd meet her daughter.

A light caress glided across the back of his hand, breaking into his bleak thoughts. In the torchlight, Imogen's features were soft with sympathy. Her fingers laced with his over the Senet board. "I am so sorry, Cededa. Was it the Waters that healed you?"

He nodded. The colossal power trapped inside a tiny stream hidden far beneath Tineroth's caves made Imogen's bane look like child's play. Burned to a mound of ash and blackened bone should have ended him. The agony he suffered during the burning made him beg for death, but even fire couldn't conquer the Waters' effects. Cededa was reborn, cinder by cinder until he stood before Niamh, whole and unmarked by his immolation, except for the memories scorched into his mind.

"The Waters are a blessing then," Imogen said.

His hand convulsed in her clasp. "Is that what you believe?"

Her grip tightened, and her gray eyes narrowed. She peered at him intently, as if searching for the right words. "No, I don't believe it. I believe you're more cursed than I am." She used her free hand in a gesture that encompassed not only the room they shared but Tineroth itself. "What blessing is there in living an immortal life caught between worlds? Alone?"

Cededa chuckled and lifted her hand, turning it to place a kiss in her palm. He could name one blessing now—he'd lived long enough to meet and fall in love with Niamh's extraordinary daughter. He lowered her hand but kept it clasped in his. "I ruled an empire, one built by my grandfather and expanded by my father, but empires are more slippery than eels and harder to control. I needed more time to expand my lands, consolidate Tineroth's power, bring other kingdoms under my rule. More time than a single mortal's lifespan."

The recollection of that far-off age, when he'd been consumed by avarice and ambition, held a pain greater than his immolation by mercenaries intent on stealing the Waters. "Imagine my joy when we discovered the Living Waters. I'd have ten lifetimes, twenty if I wished, to expand my empire. I'd be king of the world, not just the lands I'd inherited or conquered so far."

Imogen frowned. "There's nothing noble in carrying on a legacy of conquest." She eased her hand out of his grip, and he let her go.

Cededa arched an eyebrow. "You know nothing of empires, Imogen." She blushed and looked away. "A monarch who chooses ideals over power isn't a monarch for long." Experience had taught him that.

She must have caught the regret tainting his declaration. "Was it worth it? Drinking the Waters?"

"No." She made to ask another question, then closed her mouth abruptly. "Say or ask it, Imogen. No use in hiding your desire to do so."

She hesitated before forging ahead. "When did you become Cededa the Butcher?"

His insides froze at the question. He expected it, had always expected it from the moment she crossed the bridge and begged his help. Who wouldn't want to know how someone came by such a grotesque title?

He dropped his gaze to the Senet board, moved his king through her defense wall and crushed her army in the game. When he looked up once more, he caught her eyeing him warily.

"After I led soldiers into Mir and destroyed yet another rebellion. I made a lesson of the city." His voice was soft, toneless. "We left none alive."

Imogen fisted her hands in her skirts. He heard the gasp trapped in her throat. She swallowed hard. "The women?" she whispered. "Children?"

He shook his head. "None left alive," he repeated. "It took us three days. The canals and the fountains, even the river ran red with blood." Only Tineroth's screaming for his return had ever drowned out the screams of the dying that still rang in his mind.

Imogen lunged away from him, knocking the table with her knee hard enough to make the Senet board jump and spill the game pieces onto the floor. He watched, unmoving, as she scooted back on her haunches, desperate to put space between them.

The Butcher. He'd given her the truth, if not the answer she probably wanted. Not a hyperbolic title risen from the dramatic retellings of a popular fable, but a name earned and deserved. A part of him withered away at the sight of her scuttling back from him, revulsion twisting her features. He knew what she saw—the monster of legend, the reason why each of his images, except the catafalque, had been destroyed, why his people had finally revolted and why his greatest sorcerers had wrenched Tineroth from her anchor to the world and cast her into oblivion, and him along with her.

CHAPTER NINETEEN

Feeling as if she'd suffocate, Imogen lurched to her feet and bolted from the room. The palace walls and cloisters warped in her blurred vision, and she careened against a set of pilasters, nearly tumbling down the stairs in her headlong rush to escape.

As if it heard her distress, the sentient mist appeared, spilling onto the stairs, sliding under her feet and rising to encompass her in a cool cloud of faint light.

"Please, I have to get out," she implored her ghostly escort.

She cried out as the floor fell away, and she was lifted by invisible hands. They carried her to the doors and outside, setting her down gently. Imogen barely choked out a "Thank you" before collapsing on the palace steps. Tears followed; great, wrenching sobs that grew in strength until she screamed her anguish into her skirts.

Her screams turned to moans. She had bedded a monster. Called him beautiful and taken his seed into her body. The thought made her stomach heave, and she hunched over her knees, dry-retching until her ribs ached and her throat burned.

The sculptor who'd carved the effigy had known The Undying King far more than the woman who now shared his bed. Imogen wiped her cheeks on her sleeve. He hadn't told her anything she shouldn't have already guessed. He'd been named The Butcher.

Only her willful blindness had made her shy away from delving too deeply into how he'd inherited such a title.

The quiet, reserved man who skillfully and lovingly introduced her to the intimacy between man and woman and who generously offered a means by which she might live a fruitful life didn't seem the type who'd spend three days slaughtering innocents. An image of the marble effigy on the catafalque flashed in her mind's eye. The cruelty, the calculating malice—etched deep in frozen marble. That man, however, oh yes. That man would commit such atrocities and laugh as he did so.

Her tears slowed and finally dried, leaving her eyes nearly swollen shut. A dry breeze fluttered her skirts and stirred the overgrown weeds that spilled over the steps on which she sat. Behind her, the eroded hulk of one of Tineroth's many nameless buildings cast its long shadow over her and the cracked street. The memory of Niamh's words sounded in her mind like a dirge.

"His people once called him Cededa the Fair, then Cededa the Butcher, and then they called him no more."

CHAPTER TWENTY

S till seated as she left him, Cededa shoved the Senet board off the bed. "Yielded and conquered." Like all things in this interminable existence, it was a hollow triumph.

The mist that had carried Imogen outside the palace seeped into the chamber and stopped in front of Cededa. He watched as it converged and thickened, melding into the spectral form of a woman dressed in the gown of a Mir aristocrat.

Her voice was a zephyr's breeze through trees, a shifting of many voices that spoke as one. "What did you tell the girl?"

He rose from his place at the table. "I told her of Mir."

The wraith's shape changed, twisting in on itself in an agitated spiral. "She will hate you now, and she will leave."

Cededa's short huff of laughter held no humor. "She's free to go if she wishes. She has no interest in the Waters and none who'll believe her if she tells their tale. My debt to her mother will be repaid if she leaves of her own choosing."

"She can redeem you."

He smiled. "I'm beyond redemption, Gruah. You know that." He cocked his head. "When did you stop hating me?"

A ripple passed through the ghostly shape. "When you began to grieve for us, Cededa. The king you are now should have been the king to rule us then."

"A fine wisdom I realize now, four thousand years too late."

145

"Four thousand years ago, you wouldn't have listened to such wisdom."

The mist began to thin, sinking to a shapeless, swirling tide. It floated toward the door, pausing at Cededa's "Wait."

He waded into the vapor until it floated around his knees. "Will you ever forgive me for Mir, wife?"

A pale ribbon separated itself from the vaporous mass. A chilly caress drifted over Cededa's cheekbone.

"No, Sire. Such a thing isn't possible—not now."

He sighed. "Indeed."

The ribbon retreated, swallowed into the greater mist. It floated out the door, disappearing into the cloisters' shadows. Cededa followed its path until he reached the palace doors. Once outside, he surveyed the city cloaked in darkness. Imogen was nowhere in sight. Above him, the moon hid her mocking face behind a veil of clouds.

A distant sound teased his sensitive hearing. Imogen. Somewhere in Tineroth, Death's handmaiden wept for the massacred.

CHAPTER TWENTY-ONE

After crying her eyes out on the palace steps, Imogen fled into the city's heart. Two months in Tineroth and the eerie hush no longer bothered her. Now, it was a boon. There were none to wonder or remark on her flight as she made her way to the library and sat down on the toppled column Cededa had used as a seat when he first brought her here.

Imogen gave a humorless chuckle at the sight of the omnipresent mist drifting toward her. Tineroth's spectral custodian, and Imogen's watchful guard. It blanketed the steps, pausing at her feet. A sudden pressure rested against her ankle. Imogen looked down to see a full water skin next to her. She lifted it, took a healthy swallow of water and rinsed her mouth several times.

"My thanks."

She didn't expect an answer and jumped when the mist suddenly rose higher, separating itself into distinct forms that shifted and swayed with the steady breeze.

Imogen scrambled to her feet. Before her stood a virtual crowd of wraiths, their pellucid features obscured by the play of shadow and moonlight. Still, she made out what looked to be an army. Men armored for battle, helmeted and carrying both shield and sword. They hovered behind a small group of women with children at their side. A stately figure, pride evident in the set of her insubstantial shoulders, drifted closer to Imogen.

147

She raised a spectral hand and pointed to the side. Imogen followed her direction. The air rippled and shadows realigned themselves, lightening to become floating images of things that once existed in Tineroth.

Cededa as he'd once been—human, blue-eyed with sunbronzed skin. Haughty, merciless, scornful. Each trait was stamped on his sublime features. The scene changed. Tineroth, still whole but falling, her streets teeming with angry mobs and fires in the distance. Another city, razed to rubble. Blood ran in rivers down streets littered with broken bodies. A crowd of women and children huddled in a room with a vaulted ceiling. One, a stunning woman with the bearing of a queen, stood defiant before a murderous army.

The images flickered, changing twice more. Tineroth as she was now; Cededa, pale and altered by the Waters, reclined on a broken throne. The last scene had Imogen moaning behind her hand. A great bonfire with Cededa at its center, lashed to a cut timber. Silhouettes danced around the pyre, swaying drunkenly as the Undying King burned and shrieked his agony to a deaf heaven.

New tears coursed down Imogen's cheeks as the images faded. The ethereal woman raised a hand as if in farewell. The figures behind her bowed. They all shifted, losing form until they were once more a single vaporous shroud.

Imogen trailed after the mist as it led her back to the palace. Cededa waited on the lowest step, haloed in moonlight. His still features revealed nothing of his thoughts. Imogen wished she could be so unflappable.

"Who are the people in the mist?"

He gazed past her to the mist drifting away from them. "I see Gruah has revealed herself to you."

Imogen started. The last wife. The one he called his judge and punisher. "I saw soldiers, women, and children. A woman of distinction stood foremost among them. Was that Gruah?"

His mouth tightened. "Aye, it was. It is. She was a princess of Mir whose first allegiance remained with Mir. It was she who raised the rebellion against me and consorted with the Tineroth mages. Her sorcery and theirs made Tineroth as you see it now and imprisoned me here. The others were the women of her court and their children."

"And the soldiers?"

"Those who cut them down. They followed me into Mir and did my bidding. They remain in Tineroth, restless spirits who still do my bidding."

Tineroth, broken and but not entirely abandoned, only haunted. "Why do they linger here?" She scowled. "Did you raise some spell to trap their spirits?"

He matched her scowl with one of his own. "No. Before she died, Gruah cursed us all. The men loyal to me will find no rest until I do." He sighed. "But a curse demands a sacrifice of its wielder. Gruah remains with me as well, as do the women and their children who died beside her. A bargain made to insure I'd never forget what I once did."

The revulsion and horror that had consumed her earlier lessened. Cededa's light eyes almost glowed in the night's gloom. Dispassionate before, his expression was now one of abiding sorrow and regret, acknowledgement of an act that left a permanent stain on his soul. Sudden insight made her heartbeat stutter.

"My bane. You draw it from me as poison from a wound and take it onto yourself." Her eyes narrowed. "You aren't immune as you say."

His soft chuckle lacked any humor. "I didn't say that, Imogen. You did." He crossed his arms. "No, I'm not immune, only resistant and only by the Waters' grace. I die a little more each time you touch me."

"You bastard," she whispered. "You would make me your redeemer."

He'd likely been called names far fouler than "bastard" in his long life and in circumstances far more hostile, but he flinched for a moment at her insult, or maybe the betrayal in her voice. An echo of all the betrayals he participated in over the years.

"Don't flatter yourself, Imogen," he snapped. "No man, woman or god can redeem me now. Even if I'm to die, it will simply be to escape the prison of Tineroth. However, the wraiths who wait in twilight with me will find peace once I'm dead."

Imogen rubbed her eyes and looked to where the mist hovered nearby. She remembered Niamh, the silent pleading in her eyes that Imogen end her suffering with a merciful yet fatal touch. Was this so different?

She stared at Cededa, a king immortal but not invincible. A flawed, weary man. A man she loved despite all she'd just learned. "I want to go to my rooms." He stood and bowed as she passed. The weight of his gaze rested on her back long after she left him on the steps.

As usual, warm water and freshly laundered cloths awaited her. Imogen shed her skirt and tunic, bathed and slid naked beneath the bedcovers, almost numb with grief. She fell asleep, clutching the pillow Cededa had used the night before.

CHAPTER TWENTY-TWO

In the darkest hours, the Undying King entered her room on silent feet and stood sentinel by her bed, admiring her beauty. The knowledge of his sins had aged her. Fine lines marred her brow, and she muttered in her sleep.

He wanted to reach out, draw her into his embrace and somehow force her to believe that Cededa the Butcher was as dead as Cededa the Fair. Only the ghosts remained to haunt him and remind him of a past evil for which he'd never receive absolution.

As if she sensed his regard, her eyes fluttered open and she rolled to her side to face him. They gazed at one another long moments before she lifted the covers away in wordless invitation.

Forgiveness. The gesture nearly sent Cededa to his knees. He stripped and slipped beneath the covers to gather Imogen's warm body close. She spooned against him, still silent but pliant in his arms. He buried his face in her hair. The memory of her accusation echoed in his mind.

"You would make me your redeemer."

How very wrong she was. "I would make you my wife," he whispered in her ear. "My only wife. My beloved wife."

Melancholy thickened her voice, and her fingers lay cold over his. "I don't want to hate you the way they did."

His chest constricted. "I don't want that either, Imogen." He squeezed her hand. "I'm no longer that man."

"Aren't you?"

Cededa pressed on her shoulder until she lay on her back, face tilted to his. Tear tracks silvered her pale cheeks. "No, I'm not." What else was there to say?

Imogen sighed and closed her eyes. "Everything you've done in your long years, everything you feel, is part of who you are now. The question is whether or not the greater part is the man who committed atrocities or the one who regrets them."

He wanted to tell her that regret and guilt ran through his veins like death ran through hers, but he stayed silent. That question was hers to answer for herself.

Her hand drifted down his arm in a languid caress. "I never thought I'd meet a king," she said in a sleepy voice. "Especially a fabled one."

Cededa hugged her to him. Her breathing slowed, and her body grew heavy against his. "I never thought I'd hold Death," he whispered in the darkness. "Or beg her love and mercy."

CHAPTER TWENTY-THREE

Dradus's nose bled red streamers onto his silk tunic, and his skull threatened to split from the pain, but those were minor discomforts compared to the euphoria coursing through him. An ancient bridge shimmered to life under the power of complex sorcery. It stretched across the gorge, still insubstantial but solidifying with each passing moment. A bridge that connected him to fabled Tineroth and her surely substantial treasures.

The company of Castagher soldiers behind him cheered. After weeks of idle waiting while he cast spell after spell to reveal the bridge, they were restless, eager for battle and ready to conquer the city behind the heavy mists obscuring the forest on the crevasse's opposite side. Dradus nodded to the captain of the guard.

"Remember, the men are welcome to whatever loot they can carry out, but they can't forget their mission. We bring the girl back to Hayden, alive."

The captain frowned. "If she's cursed as you say, it will be a challenge to transport her.

Dradus shrugged. "A small matter. Leave it to me. Just be sure not to let her touch you when you catch her." One eyebrow rose meaningfully. "It's easy to subdue an unconscious captive."

"Aye, I see your point." The captain gestured to his troop. "I'll tell them to prepare. We ride to Tineroth at your signal."

CHAPTER TWENTY-FOUR

A familiar shrieking sent Cededa bolting out of the bed and into a dead run for the door. Tineroth's warning. Someone had breached the city's ensorcelled boundaries.

Startled awake by his abrupt movement, Imogen blinked groggily as he threw open the door and raced into the corridor. He was halfway down the stairs by the time she made it to the landing.

"Cededa, what's wrong?" Her shout didn't slow him down. He leapt the stairs three at time, heedless of his state of undress and bare feet, fueled by a towering rage that edged his vision in crimson.

"Intruders!" He called back. "Get dressed and follow Gruah. She and the others will take you to a safe place."

He sprinted to the armory. His armor waited inside, along with his favorite weaponry. Years of fighting wars made him quick and efficient at donning harness and buckling straps. He needed no squire to help him and soon stood dressed to face whoever crossed into his city uninvited.

Cededa glanced back once at the palace, hoping Imogen didn't linger there. If treasure hunters invaded the city, his palace was the worst place to hide.

Fleet and silent, he traveled along familiar streets until he reached the city's gates, open now to reveal the bridge. Cededa snarled at the sight of armed men and horses. A wizard rode in that group, one powerful enough to force the bridge into solidifying. He clenched the glaive pole he held. He'd kill the wizard first.

He waited until the horses thundered through the open gate. The city's hush exploded into a rush of shouts and motion as Cededa plunged headlong into the mass of horseflesh and men. Equine screams and agonized shouts followed his attack as his glaive sliced the air, the flashing blade cutting a bloody swathe through men and animals.

Spurred on by rage and the guardian compulsion triggered by the Waters, Cededa leapt into the air. He landed nimbly on a horse's back long enough to swing his glaive in a lethal arc, decapitating two men in a single swipe. Blood sprayed the air and him. A battle cry sounded behind him. He jumped to the ground, meeting the mounted soldier who charged him, sword raised high. The horse bore down on him in full charge. Cededa tipped the glaive, swinging it like a club so the weighted metal end slammed into the animal's forelegs. It squealed, crashing to its belly and skidding across the cobblestones. It rolled, crushing its rider beneath it.

The melee intensified. Swarmed by men and horses, Cededa plowed through the ranks, killing and maiming in a sea of carnage. He'd broken his glaive but didn't pause. The clang of metal striking metal echoed through the courtyard as he hacked and cut with axe and short sword.

He leapt over bodies, slashing his way to the back ranks milling around him in a confused chaos. Horses reared, their hooves pawing the air above his head. He shoved a soldier into the path of one of the crazed animals and heard a scream cut short by a dull thud. There were at least a score of men left, and he had every intention of killing every last one of them. He shrieked a Tineroth battle cry and slammed into their ranks with renewed fervor.

Battle frenzy roared through him, a blood heat undiminished by time. He was a warrior king bred of countless generations of warrior kings. This was his city, and he meant to defend her and the woman he claimed as his.

CHAPTER TWENTY-FIVE

Cededa's warning echoed in Imogen's ears.

Intruders? Oh gods, she prayed. Please let him be safe. The horror of his immolation would forever be emblazoned on her memory. No one, no matter their actions, should have to suffer that twice. She dressed, warning off the mist when it tried to help her. "I think not," she snapped. "I'm going fast enough."

She sensed its impatience, its concern. The spirit of Cededa's wife took form and motioned her to follow. They sped through the palace, navigating dizzying twists and turns that left Imogen disoriented and hopelessly lost. She finally emerged through a service door and into an enclosed bailey. The mist no longer gently roiled as before but shot across the bailey and into the street with Imogen sprinting to keep up.

It led her through winding closes as labyrinthine as the palace halls. They entered one of the multistoried buildings. This one was more derelict than most, with half the stairwell crumbled away and the upper floors inaccessible. Or so she assumed.

Imogen swallowed a startled gasp as invisible hands lifted and carried her upward. The vaporous mist surged over her legs and waist, enveloping her in an icy embrace before setting her down in the topmost room. Just as quickly it rolled back toward the door, pausing only a moment for Gruah to materialize once more and make a gesture that could only be interpreted as an imperative "Stay here."

It slid out the door, disappearing from view. Unless someone possessed the ability to leap nearly two stories to the nearest stair, Imogen remained out of reach. Likewise, unless she wanted to fall two stories, she was effectively trapped.

She ran to the window and nearly cried out at the scene before her. At this height, she had a clear view of the city gates. The bridge had reappeared, stretching across the empty space between the cliff walls. Horses and mounted riders thundered across the span, armor flashing in the sun. Concealed by the mist but clear to her from this side of the gorge, Cededa waited in the center of the massive courtyard just inside the city gates, a solitary defender against impossible numbers. His chainmail shone a dull silver in the morning light, and he leaned on his glaive with all the casualness of a man about to greet an old comrade instead of a hostile force.

The invaders galloped through the gates, and Cededa transformed into a shrieking demon of slicing blades and fury. Bile rose in her throat when he swung the glaive in a back swing. The curved hook behind the blade caught the metal collar of a soldier's armor, yanking the man off his horse and peeling his hauberk off him like an orange rind. Merciless, ruthless and giving no quarter, Cededa brought the glaive down and was instantly doused in blood.

Sickened and horrified by the growing slaughter, Imogen didn't notice when the door behind her opened and a silent figure crept in. Her only warning came too late—the scrape of a sole on the dusty floor. She turned in time to catch a glimpse of a man's gaunt, vulpine face before he struck her with a gloved fist. Black stars exploded behind her eyes, and she saw nothing else.

CHAPTER TWENTY-SIX

S haken by the ferocity of the Undying King's attack on his forces, Dradus fled the battle and took refuge in the shadow of a temple. Visions of finding treasure houses filled with gold faded before the white-faced juggernaut decimating his troop. Hayden would have to accept the idea his cousin and the trade agreements tied to her were lost. Dradus's only interest now was creeping out of Tineroth with his head still attached to his shoulders.

All his machinations revived when he caught a glimpse of dark hair fluttering from a high window and a woman's hands gripping the window frame. Niamh's cursed fosterling. It had to be, but even if she wasn't, it mattered little. She dwelt in a sheltered building, a sure sign she was of value to the Tineroth king.

With the aid of a few spells, it had been easy enough to reach the upper floor, despite the broken staircase. Cursed or not, he took no chances and struck her unconscious. He eyed her, crumpled at his feet. This was indeed the long lost princess of Berberi. Others might not see the resemblance, but Dradus had been an advisor to Hayden's family for many years. He recognized Selene's features in the shape of her daughter's mouth and her stubborn chin.

He lifted her, careful not to touch any part of her where bare skin was exposed. He dragged her limp frame to the window. Outside, the fighting continued unabated. Dradus incanted another spell, and his voice thundered across the city, sending the already panicked horses into a frenzy.

"King Cededa!"

The entire courtyard froze, as if caught in the spell's enchantment. Bloodied axe and sword still in hand, Cededa half crouched, prepared to face off against his next opponent.

He took a running leap, cleared several bodies of horses and men, and raced for the temple, a murderous rage evident in his stride. He halted when Dradus jerked Imogen's head back, exposing her pale throat to a knife's blade.

The mage smiled, triumphant. He was right. He possessed the bargaining chip that might well get him and what remained of his troop out of Tineroth alive. A good thing he was skilled at bluffing. If the king even suspected he had no intention of killing his hostage, they were all dead.

"Put down your weapons, Your Majesty and surrender. Otherwise I kill her."

Cededa eyed Dradus for a long moment, and even from the safety of both height and distance, Dradus shuddered under the touch of that cold-blooded gaze.

Axe and sword fell at Cededa's feet with a discordant clang. Those Castagher soldiers still alive and uninjured closed around him. He didn't fall at the first punch or even the third kick. By the sixth, he was on his knees. At a dozen, he fell and lay still, bloodied and defeated.

CHAPTER TWENTY-SEVEN

Imogen wakened to a splitting headache and the rhythmic creak of wheels. She cracked open one eye, squinting as the light worsened the throbbing in her skull. As she grew more alert, she discovered her hands wrapped and bound, every part of her skin once bared now covered. She sat up slowly, startled when a man in dented armor struck the side of the wagon and ordered her to be still.

Oh gods, the invaders. Horses and injured men surrounded the rickety wagon in which she rode. A river roared beneath them, and the statues of the ancient Tineroth kings loomed above her as the procession marched across the bridge and away from the city.

She pushed herself up, ignoring the same soldier's harsh reprimands, gaze sweeping the crowd in search of Cededa. If the gods answered prayers, he remained safe in the city.

Her prayers went unanswered. She glimpsed flashes of pale hair splashed with red in the group following her wagon.

Imogen tottered to her feet and jumped from the wagon. The men walking behind it leapt out of her way as she rolled on the hard stone. Gasping from the shock of hitting unforgiving ground, she stood, swaying unsteadily. "Cededa!" Her cry echoed over the wind whistling across the bridge and the river thundering below it.

Stripped to just his trews, the Undying King had been reduced to a stumbling wreck of bruises and welts. Purple and black patterns of fists and boot heels mottled his torso, and his hair stuck to a battered and bloodied face. He lurched behind a horse, tethered to the saddle by a length of rope that cinched his wrists so tightly blood trickled under the knots. The rider yanked on the rope, sending Cededa to his knees where he was dragged across the rough stone until he gained his feet once more.

"Stop it!" Imogen wove an unsteady path toward her lover. "Let him stand!"

She never reached him. A firm hand on her elbow whirled her about so that she faced the man who'd struck her senseless. He bowed briefly, eyes icy with both curiosity and disdain.

"He's of no concern to you any more, Your Highness. Please return to the wagon."

Imogen stared at the stranger, angered and astonished. What was he talking about? This man had hit her hard enough to rearrange her eyes and now he addressed her as if she were royalty. While his expression held only contempt, his voice was one of deference and civility. Had the world gone mad?

"Get your hands off me," she snarled and yanked her arm out of his grip. The soldiers who'd jumped out of her way earlier closed ranks again, blocking her view of Cededa.

She wrestled the stranger as he grabbed around the waist and hauled her back to the wagon. Her desperation to reach the king gave her added strength but she was still no match for her captor. He slung her none too gently in the wagon. Red-faced and breathing hard, he glared at her.

"Be still, Highness, or I'll be forced to do what I did in Tineroth."

Imogen gathered every bit of moisture in her mouth and spat. He was quicker than she expected and dodged her shot. "Do that again, and I'll gag you."

She opened her mouth to hurl at him every epithet she'd overheard in the marketplaces but halted at a panicked cry from the end of the procession.

"The bridge! It's fading! Run!"

Chaos ensued as those in the back of the line surged forward, crowding those closer to the front. Imogen's captor leapt into the wagon with her and shouted at the driver to move it. The wagon bounced and rattled. Imogen held on to one side as it careened from right to left, knocking against horses that raced for the safety of the land. In the mayhem, the orderly ranks of marching men broke as they ran with the horses for safety. The rider holding Cededa's rope raced past them, his captive no longer tethered.

Imogen saw him then, standing alone and still as the bridge vanished behind him. "Cededa!" She screamed his name, stretching out her bound arms as if she might catch him before the span disappeared beneath his feet. His bloodied mouth turned up in an enigmatic smile, and his voice whispered to her over the thunder of hooves.

"Farewell, my beauty."

Her desolate cry carried through the gorge as the bridge disappeared and Cededa fell silently into the chasm to the river below.

CHAPTER TWENTY-EIGHT

Summer lay fully upon Castagher. Imogen stood on her balcony and watched the sun set on the harbor. She'd never been this close to the sea before and admired the way the water turned to liquid fire in the sun's reflective light. Ships rocked on languid waves, and farther out, in open water, Castagher traded on its newly acquired shipping lanes.

A door opened and closed behind her, alerting her to a visitor. She recognized the click of her cousin's boots on the floor and braced herself. "I'm out here, Your Majesty," she called to him.

The clicking grew louder, accompanied by the scent of rosemary and beeswax candles. Imogen turned to Hayden as he took his place beside her. Charming, handsome, and with a sharp wit, Hayden of Castagher oozed insincerity. His overtures of friendship rang false, and his gaze on her made her feel like a moth trapped in a spider's web.

"Out on the balcony again, I see."

She summoned a smile with effort. "I have one of the best views in the city. Seems a shame to waste it."

He acknowledged her compliment by preening. "True, but can't you find a moment to join me in the main hall? We've a talented bard to entertain us at supper and a harpist from Minos. The best harpists come out of Minos, you know."

Imogen honestly didn't care if the harpist came from the royal stables and brought fiddlers from the catacombs with them.

They'd had this conversation in various incarnations several times. Hayden had tried to coax her out of her room and join him with his court in the great hall.

She indulged him once, and that had been enough to know she was feared by the courtiers and unwelcomed in their midst. Her curse, weakened by Cededa's touch, had returned full strength once she left Tineroth. Even had she been made free of Niamh's bane, none would trust her enough to test it. While she found the courtiers' reactions to her a perfect excuse to avoid meals in the royal hall, she was more isolated and alone in Castagher's court than she'd ever been in her life.

"Please extend my apologies. You know I'm uncomfortable around so many people in one place. Nor are they comfortable around me."

Hayden's mouth thinned. "They'll hold their tongues if they know what's good for them." He sighed and leaned against the balcony's ledge. "You're a lot like your mother, you know. She had this sweetness about her. A sweetness that hid a stubbornness worthy of a mule."

Imogen offered him a tight smile. She'd known early on that she was Niamh's fosterling, and while she'd been curious about her parents, her foster mother's distress at the questions she asked had made her reluctant to push for more. Niamh had been a strong and giving parent despite the dark beginning they shared between them. Only now, learning of her through Hayden's recollections, did Imogen regret not knowing Selene.

Unlike the rest of his court, Hayden showed no fear of her touch. He grasped her gloved hand and bent to kiss her knuckles.

A cold shiver made her fingers twitch. "If you change your mind, tell your maid. Someone will escort you to the hall."

"Thank you, cousin." *Now go away.*

He paused at the balcony doors. "Solstice will be here in a few days. Castagher celebrates with a festival by the water. I want to take you there." He frowned. "You can't stay in your rooms forever, Imogen. Consider my invitation." A threat and a command wrapped in silky words.

Imogen nodded. "I will." She waited until he closed the door behind him to wipe her hand on her skirts.

Solstice. She had great plans for that day. Despite the trappings of luxury and privilege, she was a prisoner of Castagher and Hayden her jailer. He had sent soldiers to abduct her and bring her to him. She had been the proof he required to claim rights of trade from Berberi, the bride promised to him when he was merely a child and she a babe hardly a week old.

She had listened, numb, when he explained why a small army had scoured two kingdoms to find her and deliver her to his care. Even his knowledge of her curse didn't deter him from planning their union. She wasn't a beloved bride, merely a means to an end, as many aristocratic women were in matters of marriage.

She despised Hayden for his single-minded ambition and casual disregard of her feelings, but she reserved her greatest loathing for Dradus, his sorcerer. Sly, deceptive and calculating, he made Imogen's skin crawl with revulsion. He'd earned her enmity when he used her to break Cededa, intensifying it to hatred when he revealed how he found her on their return trip to Castagher.

"I raised Niamh's body from the grave for a little chat." He smirked at her horrified inhalation. "You can learn a lot of from the dead if you ask the right questions. The witch told me where to find you."

"You're fouler than the bottom of a privy pit," Imogen spat. "I hope she curses you from her grave."

His smirked deepened. "Like she cursed you?" Imogen froze, and the smirk turned to a full-blown shark's grin. "She didn't tell you, did she? Took her secret to the grave." Dradus folded his hands under his chin. "Niamh of Leids became the castoff mistress of King Varn when he married your mother. A woman scorned is a dangerous creature; a sorceress scorned, a lethal one. She laid a death geas on your parents, but something went wrong, and you inherited the curse. You killed two wet nurses, a maid and your parents before someone figured out you were the assassin."

Imogen wondered when all the air had suddenly been sucked out of the room. She couldn't breathe. Dradus watched her with a reptilian gaze and the smirk she so badly wanted to strike off his face with one killing blow. "You're lying," she said. "Niamh would never cast such a geas, if only because she loved me and liked children. She'd never put me at such risk."

She did believe; however, in her foster mother's need for revenge. Niamh's journal revealed how much she loved Varn. Broken-hearted, enraged, she might well have sought vengeance against him and the woman he took to wife.

The mage shook his head. "Niamh didn't know Selene was pregnant. When she discovered what happened and that Varn's sister planned to have you drowned, she stole you away and disappeared."

Niamh, who had devoted her life to raising and protecting Imogen, had been the reason for her curse. Tears clouded her vision, and Imogen forced them back. Never would she cry before this piece of filth.

Her foster mother had begged her for forgiveness on her deathbed. Deep inside, where Dradus couldn't see, Imogen wept. For herself and a life so profoundly altered by another woman's revenge, for Niamh who willingly sentenced herself to raising a child who wielded death in her touch, and for the parents she never knew who welcomed their firstborn into the world and died because of it.

Imogen had fled Dradus's presence and avoided him now as much as possible. Hayden favored him; she wished him dead and remained wary whenever they crossed paths. His questions regarding Tineroth and Cededa held all manner of traps designed to catch a slip of the tongue or glean a secret. Imogen silently thanked Cededa for never telling her where the Living Waters pooled in Tineroth. Dradus would get nothing from her.

He often told Hayden his studies called him to other cities and towns, and he disappeared for several days, returning with a frustrated scowl and more probing questions for Imogen. She suspected he returned to the gorge in the futile hope of resurrecting the Yinde Bridge and a second crossing into Tineroth. He believed Cededa dead, killed by his own magic and the river that accepted his plummeting body. Imogen didn't naysay him, though she fervently hoped he was wrong.

All her plans, her desires, her reason for not falling into despair rested in the belief that Cededa had survived and returned to Tineroth.

She abandoned the balcony for her room. Long shadows stretched across the floor, and her maid Lila circled the room, lighting lamps to chase away the darkness. She eyed her mistress as one might a barely tamed beast—cautious and ready to take flight at the first hint of attack.

Imogen quelled the urge to roll her eyes. Lila was no different from any of the others. Her fear of Imogen's curse hadn't lessened with time or Imogen's friendly overtures. She curtsied nervously, nearly setting her skirts on fire with the lit candle she carried.

"'Good evening, Your Highness. Will you be wanting your supper in your room tonight?"

The question was virtually rhetorical at this point. Since she'd first arrived at Castagher, Imogen had only eaten in the feasting hall once, an interminable evening characterized by rude stares, whispers and insincere smiles.

"Yes, Lila. Thank you."

The maid bobbed another curtsey before fleeing the chamber. Imogen waited until the door closed before pulling a travel sack from under her bed. In it she'd stuffed a water flask, a few days' worth of pilfered oat cakes and a dress discarded by the palace's head laundress. To these, she added a heavy cloak and a small purse containing four skells of silver, enough to buy a horse and ride to the Castagheri border. The sack went back under the bed. Thank the gods her maids were lazy and didn't bother to dust under there. All she could do now was wait.

The days before Solstice crawled on feeble legs. The entire city prepared to celebrate, and for once Hayden didn't insist Imogen join him in the upcoming celebrations. Death's handmaiden among a drunken crowd of celebrants presented too much of a risk. Imogen occupied herself with studying the map she had tucked away in a book of poems. She had memorized every detail but studied it a final time before tossing it in the fireplace's grate where the flames greedily devoured the parchment.

She thought of Niamh once more. She might have discounted Dradus's revelations as lies, but Hayden verified most of them.

Stricken by her lover's change of affections from his mistress to his new wife, Niamh had gone mad. The need for vengeance had overridden any sense of reason or compassion, and she'd leveled a dark power against King Varn's wife, never knowing until too late that her bane had stricken the unborn child Selene carried.

Death ran like blood through Imogen's tiny hands, striking down any she touched, including Selene, Varn, the midwife and nursemaids. By the time Niamh discovered the devastation her curse had wrought, Varn's sister had stepped in and instructed the newborn be taken out of the castle and drowned in the nearest well. The maid assigned to the hideous task never saw the blow that struck her down or the fleet shadow that gently lifted the sleeping infant from her cradle and vanished with her into the night.

Imogen refused to cry in front of Dradus, but she sobbed alone in her room until the tears ran dry. That night she dreamed of Cededa and his wraith wife Gruah. Gruah held out a nebulous hand, wispy fingers curling around Imogen's. In the dream, she spoke and her voice chimed like tiny bells in a summer garden. "Yours is a great heart, Imogen. Can you forgive?"

The next morning she woke, a lightness and renewed sense of purpose filling her. Now, she sat on her bed, dressed in castoffs with her journey sack near her feet. She'd forgone gloves as being too distinctive. Instead, she buried her hands in her pockets and prayed none would put her in a position that she'd accidently touch them. A linen kerchief covered her hair, and she practiced slouching so as to appear shorter than she was. With any luck, those still awake in the castle were either too drunk on wine or too sleepy to recognize her.

The night sky was slowly paling as she sneaked out of her room and tiptoed down the hall toward the back staircase used by the servants. Only the head cook and a scullery maid were awake, and they remained in the kitchen.

Imogen's luck held as she navigated a path through Castagher to her fortified walls and finally past the gates to the post stables where the horses for hire were kept. The stable master leered at her but didn't question where a laundress had gotten the funds to rent a horse. Within the hour, she was galloping toward the borders shared by Castagher and Berberi on a mount too old and knackered to care that it carried death on its back. If her luck stayed with her, she would reach the gorge in three days' time.

The miles flew by as they traveled steadily toward Tineroth. Imogen measured the distance and counted the hours. Solstice was almost here. Desperation grew within her. Reaching the gorge was the easy part. Reaching Tineroth before it vanished from the world, another thing altogether.

She left the horse at a stable in a village bordering the forest. The wood welcomed her, a shelter of dappled shade and relief from the hot sun. Imogen traveled south on foot through thick underbrush and reached the gorge at twilight. Across the gorge's empty space concealing mist parted briefly to reveal the flickering, shadowy outlines of buildings. Home.

Unfortunately, she no longer had a key to unlock the door or summon the bridge that would carry her across the divide.

A far off sound drifted to her ears. The voices of men calling, the unmistakable resonant baying of dogs tracking their quarry.

"No," she breathed. Surely, Hayden hadn't noticed her gone or tracked her so soon! Dradus's vulpine features rose in her mind, and she growled. "You rat bastard. You set a spy on me."

Imogen paced along the cliff's edge. She had nowhere to run. Besides, she had only one place in mind she wanted to be, and at the moment it was out of reach. She picked up a rock and threw it over the cliff's edge in frustration. "Cededa!" She shouted, uncaring if the hunting pack heard her.

The dogs' baying grew louder with renewed excitement. Imogen threw another rock. "Cededa!" This time her bellow carried far across the divide. Still nothing from the other side. A terrible fear nearly consumed her. What if the immortal king had not survived the fall into the river? What if Tineroth no longer held her last living son captive?

More shouts behind her, this time close enough she expected to see horses and dogs burst from the forest understory at any moment.

"Cededa!" She shrieked his name a third time. There'd be no fourth time. Dradus's hunters were almost on top of her.

Tears blurred her vision, an impotent fury born of frustration and despair threatening to consume her. Suddenly the air in front of her wavered, rolling and shimmering. The Yinde bridge took shape, vague but solid enough. At the other end a pale figure waited, and Imogen cried out, exultant.

Her euphoria died a quick death when a shaggy-haired hound broke from the trees and loped toward her. Dradus's command of "Catch her!" urged it to a faster pace.

"Run, Imogen."

Cededa's cool voice carried on the wind, and Imogen's feet grew wings. She dashed across the bridge, feeling it dissolve almost immediately under her feet. If she stumbled, she'd plummet to her death. Behind her, a cacophony of howls and curses rent the air. Imogen took a running leap, landing hard enough in Cededa's arms that he grunted and staggered backwards, almost losing his balance.

Imogen wrapped her arms and legs around his body, uncaring that she nearly knocked him to the ground. He lived. Still bound, still trapped but here, waiting for her.

CHAPTER TWENTY-NINE

Cededa ignored the hue and cry of Imogen's pursuers and carried her into the shelter of Tineroth's forest. She clutched him as if she were drowning, her legs around his waist, her face buried in his shoulder.

The shock of seeing her, throwing rocks and shrieking his name, hadn't left him. When he collapsed the bridge and fell into the chasm, he thought his last memory of her would be the horror in her expression at watching him fall. Half drowned and beaten, with Tineroth's voice screaming in his head, he'd returned to the city. The familiar hush enveloped him at the gates, along with the ghostly mist that helped him into the palace to Imogen's chambers. He collapsed in her bed, where he healed and tried to forget her.

Now, the improbable had happened. She was in Tineroth once more, in his arms where she belonged. Neither spoke as he carried her into the palace and to the chambers he now thought of as hers. Clothing was tossed aside to fall in scattered piles near the bed. He was inside her before they even fell back to the mattress.

She was slick and hot and tight, gripping his cock with inner muscles that flexed and drew him deeper inside her. Imogen groaned into his mouth, opening hers wider to receive his tongue and suck his in return.

She slid her hands into his hair, holding him close, as if terrified he might fade in her arms. Theirs was a quick, primal mating of desperate caresses and hard thrusts. Cededa groaned her name, shuddering as his climax surged a shockwave of pleasure through his limbs. His fingers continued to tease and coax Imogen until she followed, arching against him with a thin cry.

Cededa barely gave her time to catch her breath before he rolled onto his back, carrying her with him. He rested inside her, still partially erect. She stroked strands of his pale hair away from his forehead and cheek, her gaze touching on each hollow and line of his features.

"You were a bloody mess when I last saw you," she said.

"I'm none the worse for it now."

"Thank the gods," she whispered and kissed his mouth.

For weeks he had raged at his imprisonment, his inability to hunt down her captors and rescue her. He had lost any hope of seeing her again and feared she suffered a brutal fate from those who'd taken her. All he could do was strengthen the wards that resisted outsider magic and prevented the bridge from taking shape unless he commanded it.

Now, Imogen lay in his arms, content and smiling. Wherever the wizard and soldiers had taken her, she'd been treated well.

"Why are you here, Imogen?"

"Because you're here." She planted soft kisses on his cheeks, his hairline. "I want to stay. You are home to me and so is Tineroth."

Cededa sighed and closed his eyes. Near dead hope rose within him. He shoved it back, wary of her declaration, her youth. He didn't doubt her sincerity, only her far sight. "Imogen, Tineroth hasn't been home to anyone except me and a crowd of revenants for four millennia. It's derelict, isolated and by this time tomorrow, will vanish from the living world until another thieving mage finds a way to drag her back." He stroked the slope of her shoulder, admiring the feel of her smooth skin under his palm. "You're very young. You don't know what you ask."

His eyes widened when she slapped him lightly on the shoulder and scowled. "Don't patronize me, Cededa. I am young, but just because it took you a few thousand years to learn and get it right doesn't mean it will take me so long."

He grinned, too pleased with her indignant protest to take offense. He turned serious once more. "When Tineroth vanishes, she will be caught between worlds, frozen in time. The stars appearing in the night sky now won't be there tomorrow night. Days and nights will be nothing more than a fading and brightening of light. No change of seasons. No rain. Do you understand what I'm saying, Imogen? There is a sameness here to drive the strongest person mad. Some would say I'm halfway there already, and they'd be right. You'd face the same thing if you stayed here with me."

He watched her face as she mulled over his words. "I'm a princess of Castagher," she said, startling Cededa with that bit of information. "But I'd rather be a queen of Tineroth."

"And rule beside me over the dead and forgotten?" He refused to soften the reality of his existence in Tineroth. If she stayed with him, she'd share that reality. He wanted no misconceptions between them.

Her eyes darkened. "Fitting, I think. My bane is still with me."

He sighed, his fear confirmed. "Aye, I thought it might be. Niamh's belief in my powers was misplaced. I can only lessen the effects, not rid you of them entirely."

"Then I'd say that's a reason as good as any for me to stay with you. Maybe by the time you've leached enough of this malice out of my blood, we'll both be old and can die together."

"Imogen..."

She stopped his protest with a kiss. "Let me stay," she implored. "Let me love you. I know you love me. Whether it's for one lifetime or six, give us both that time, that chance."

He shivered, hardly daring to trust in her declaration. Theirs wouldn't be a normal life, but neither had led such a life before. This one, with her as his companion, had the potential for being better than most. And she loved him—had told him so in a matter-of-fact way that left no room for doubt. She had abandoned a new life of rank and privilege to return to him. What more proof could he ask of her devotion?

She squealed when he held her tight enough to crush the breath out of her lungs. "Six lifetimes isn't enough, Imogen," he teased. "I'm a demanding king. I'd want at least a hundred." He kissed her softly and stared into her eyes. "I will love you until we are both dust, when even Tineroth is no more and passes from all memory."

Her eyes grew glossy with tears. "Is that all?" she croaked. She grinned and cleared her throat. "How inconstant of you."

Cededa laughed and flipped her onto her back, tickling her until Imogen shrieked for him to stop. When they settled amidst a twist of linens, he kissed her slowly, drugging kisses that had her pushing against him, demanding more of him. He complied, raising her hips to accept him. Her contented sigh echoed his as he possessed her once more.

"Welcome home, wife," he whispered.

~END~

ABOUT THE AUTHOR

Grace Draven is a fan of fantasy worlds, romance, and the anti-hero. Storytelling has been a long-standing passion of hers and a perfect excuse for not doing the laundry. She lives in Texas with her husband, three kids and big, doofus dog. You can check out her latest projects at www.gracedraven.com.

58443304R00106

Made in the USA
Lexington, KY
10 December 2016